Book Dedication

A Passion For Classic Cars
A Fleur De Lys Book

First Published in Great Britain 2016 by Fleur De Lys Publishing
Reprinted with minor revisions 2017
www.fleurdelyspublishing.com

British Library Cataloguing-in-Publication Data
A catalogue record for this book is available on request from the British
Library.

ISBN 978-0-9560298-5-0

Set in 11pt Adobe Garamond Pro by Fleur De Lys in house typesetting.

A Passion For Classic Cars

~ The Sex Story ~

by Jude Calvert-Toulmin

www.fleurdelyspublishing.com
judecalverttoulmin.com

Keep love in your heart. A life without it is like a sunless garden when the flowers are dead. ~ Oscar Wilde

For my husband Brian Trevelyan

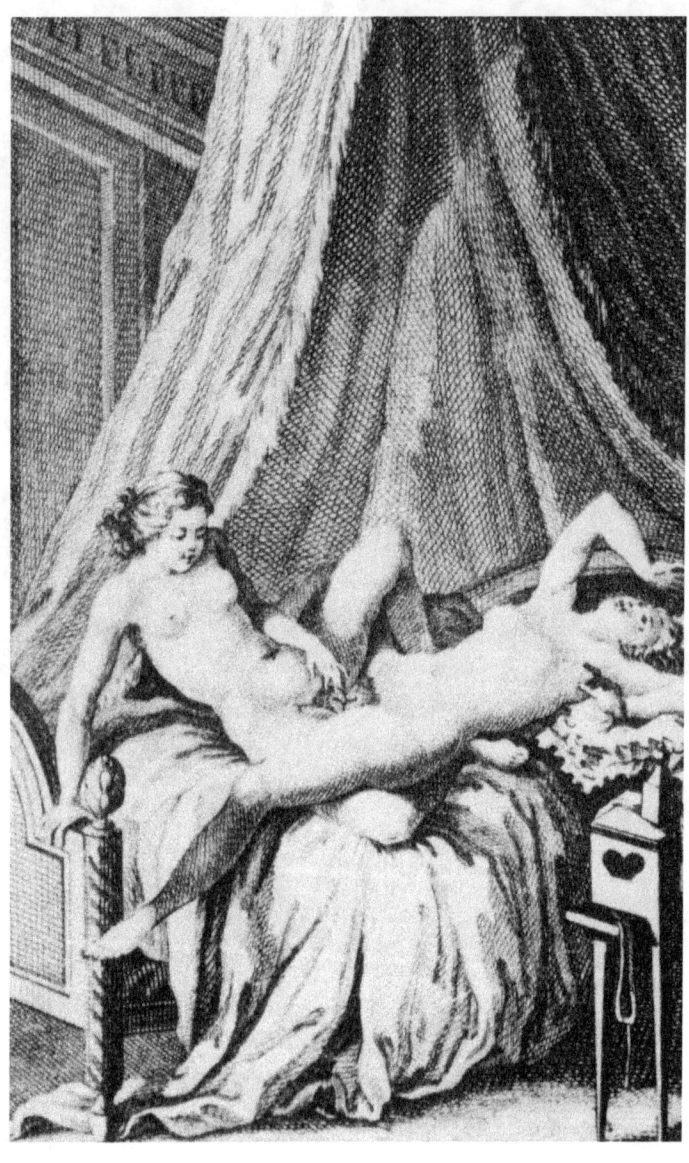

Engraving by Borel and Elluin, Mémoires de Saturnin~1787

Letter to the Reader

ear Reader,

Eighteen months ago my life was transformed. A successful novelist of crime fiction, my life was far from being a whirl of glittering glamour. After my husband Jack died, I was living the clichéd life of the lonely widow.

Until I fell in love with my son-in-law, Alex, and he fell in love with me.

Naturally it caused uproar in the family. I'm not an immoral person, and because my daughter Kate, Alex's wife, was already having an affair, Alex and I felt we weren't betraying anyone.

Kate couldn't handle it of course and has barely spoken to me since. I think what annoyed her most about everything was her affair with Colin never worked out...I've never met him... he sounded like a complete arsehole.

But then she got together with male model, Matt, whom apparently Colin hates. They've been living together ever since and she's happy, so why is she still angry with me? Oh god, I don't know. She hasn't grown out of blaming the parents I guess. It's not like she and Alex were madly in love and I snatched him from under her nose, is it?

If you want to read it as it happened, it's all in my memoirs, Mother-in-Law, Son-in-Law, which I wrote eighteen months ago. If you want to know what happened next, keep reading...

With love and affection,
Julia xxx

A Passion for Classic Cars

1

BAD SEX

lex: 'It was a dark and stormy night'...start it like that.

Julia: I can't. Taboo. Verboten. Any novel that starts 'It was a dark and stormy night' is doomed to failure.

Alex: Like saying the word 'Macbeth' instead of 'The Scottish Play'?

Julia: No. Because it's a crap way to start a book, Alex.

Alex rolls over, away from Julia and reaches out for his glass of whisky, takes a slug, puts the glass down then rolls back towards Julia again.

Alex: But you write crime fiction. It's a fitting start to a crime novel.

Julia: Stop being silly. I have to start books in my own way.

Alex: But Mrs Bridgewater, I like to give you ideas... suggestions...

Alex slides his hand across Julia's shoulder, white in the reflection of the moonlight and cool from the breeze drifting in through the open window. Then he moves his hand under the sheet, sliding his hand over Julia's breast, cupping its weight in his palm and massaging her warm, silky skin, finally running his fingers over her erect nipple.

Her long, wavy blonde hair fans out over her shoulder and onto the white pillow. Her heart-shaped face looks innocent and tired and her perfect, turned-up nose makes her look sweet and vulnerable. Alex looks into her eyes and she smiles.

Alex: Eighteen months we've been together and I don't fancy you any less.

Julia: Ditto. You're gorgeous Alex.

Julia turns to face Alex. Six feet two, curly brown hair which falls to just below his neckline and the face of an angel, like the face on a Michelangelo Greek statue. She pulls the sheet completely away from him, exposing his body. She runs her eyes downwards from his face. His torso is perfectly toned, smooth, hairless and slightly tanned. His cock is large and is sticking upright in a stiff erection.

Julia lightly brushes his chest with her fingers then puts the flat of her palm across the end of his penis, rubbing slightly across the moist, shiny head. Immediately she's aroused, and squeezes her thighs together with pleasure. Alex cups both of her breasts in his hands. Where did this myth arise that older women have saggy breasts? Julia's breasts are lush, firm and heavy, he holds them together, leans over and buries his face in them, sighing heavily.

His cock is pressing against her belly now. Julia slides her hand down and grasps the length of it firmly in her right hand then starts pumping the shaft gently. Alex sighs, closes his eyes and parts his lips slightly.

Julia: I want you now, Alex. I can't wait.

Alex opens his eyes and looks at Julia's beautiful face, her eyes radiant, her lips smiling, leans over and kisses her deeply on her mouth. Her tongue is soft and melting, already he can't wait any longer to be inside her and rolls her over onto her back, moves on top of her and reaches down to guide his stiff penis into her pussy.

Julia opens her legs and feels his cock parting her and pushing deep inside her. She gasps with pleasure and looks at Alex's face. His eyes are closed and he starts pumping inside her with fast, deep thrusts. The brown curls of hair framing his face tremble as he moves and she feels vulnerable, liquid and completely open as he fucks her.

She reaches down with one hand and gently cups his balls, and with the other hand pulls him even deeper inside her. His rhythm is getting faster and faster and Julia holds him as close as she can, until he gasps with his orgasm and Julia feels a reassuring flood of warmth inside her from his semen.

Alex collapses onto Julia's chest and she closes her eyes, listening to his deep breathing. After a couple of minutes he lifts his head up and looks at her.

Alex: You didn't come.
Julia: It doesn't matter.
Alex: Let me make you come. Or do you want to make yourself come?
Julia: No, it's fine.
Alex: Let me make Mrs Bridgewater come, pretty please?

Julia gently pushes Alex off her and sighs deeply, looking out of the window at the cloudless night, little stars and planets pinpricking the darkness outside with gold.

Julia: Alex, really, it's fine. I'm not bothered. Maybe I'm just not in the mood.

Alex: I *thought* your mind wasn't on it.

Julia: So why didn't you stop?

Alex: You seemed to be enjoying it.

Julia: I *was!*

Alex: But not properly.

Julia: I was wet, wasn't I? Proof that I was enjoying it...ready...

Alex: But you weren't...giving off that heat that you give off when you're really aroused...

Julia: Sorry. I suppose you're right. Mentally, I wasn't in the mood.

Alex: Is it me?

⁂

'Yes, Alex, it's you!' I want to scream. I'm fed up with your stupid jokes, your childishness, your little quips. Calling me 'Mrs Bridgewater' which is a bad hangover from that lovey-dovey phase of pet name-calling which is over now.

He's lying there, sipping his whisky, smiling to himself, off in some reverie and not really here with me. How is that meant to arouse me? I *was* aroused though. Well, the sight of his cock is *bound* to arouse me. But it arouses me *despite* myself. I am no longer mentally aroused by him. So why are we still together?

Alex reaches over for his iPhone, plugs his headphones into his ears and starts watching some rock climbing video. That's another thing. His climbing's gone right out the window. He used to take me to the Peak District, long golden autumn afternoons, making love in a quiet recess of the crag in the slanting afternoon sunlight. Where did that go? The new job. That's when everything changed, when he left the small independent Liquid Fire and joined the conglomerate, Bates &

Bartle. Corporate web design. It doesn't suit him. He never used to stay at the office till ten at night. Now he's rarely home at teatime. In fact, when's the last time we had a sit-down meal together during the week? But even when we do. God Julia, *don't go there*. No, *do* go there. *Go there. Admit it*. You're *bored* with him, aren't you? He *bores* you! When did he get boring? It's his age. Thirty-one is still a kid. I'm fed up with *mothering* him, that's what it is. He's so fucking *stupid* sometimes.

Alex: *Awesome!*

No, Alex, it's not awesome. It's boring.

⁊⁊⁊

What the fuck is wrong with her? I've just shagged her, haven't I? OK she didn't come but what am I meant to do if she won't let me do anything about it? She used to love me going down on her. Now she doesn't even seem bothered about having an orgasm. Maybe it's her *age*. Don't go there Alex. You *love* Julia, remember? You're *in love with Julia*, right? She just doesn't seem to be bothered about sex though. I know she's going through the menopause...maybe that's it. But she was going through the menopause when I met her and she couldn't get enough of me then! Well it's not me. I know it's not me. I know because of...no don't. Don't think about that...

⁊⁊⁊

Julia: You know, I'm really pissed off with Kate.

Alex is smiling at the iPhone screen as some young climber takes a fall and bounces around on the end of his rope.

Alex: Nearly nailed it, dude. Nearly.

Julia stares at Alex and he glances at her, sees the look on her face and removes his headphones.

Alex: Did you say something?
Julia: Yes. I said 'I'm pissed off with Kate.'
Alex: What's new there? I've been pissed off with her for the last eight years.
Julia: Don't slag her off, Alex. She's my daughter, remember.
Alex: You're slagging her off.
Julia: No, I'm not. I'm saying I'm pissed off with her.
Alex: Why? What is it now?
Julia: The same as usual. Matt. Eighteen months they've been together and she still won't introduce us to him.
Alex: Maybe she's frightened you'll do what you did with me and snatch him from right under her nose.
Julia: Don't be ridiculous. It's not that.
Alex: Well I don't know, do I? We could theorise all day as to why she won't introduce him.
Julia: Yes, we could. It's called 'Having a conversation' Alex and women enjoy doing it as much as they enjoy sex! Do you want to talk about this or not?
Alex: Don't be like that. Of course I do. What do you think the problem is, then?
Julia: She's still angry about you and me. So she's trying to lead a separate life.
Alex: She seems OK when you and her go shopping together.
Julia: That's because I'm buying her things.
Alex: That makes sense. Typical Kate.

Julia: But she won't come round here, because of you, and she won't bring Matt when I meet her in London. She's just being... subversive. Awkward. To punish me.

Alex: As always. Look, Julia, she's a grown woman. I've said it millions of times, you have to just let her go and allow her to live her own life. You can't keep trying to control her.

Julia: I'm *not* trying to control her! It would just be *nice* if we could meet her live-in boyfriend, *that's all!*

Alex: Do we really give a fuck?

Julia: Yes, Alex, *I do* give a fuck. And my opinion counts. It's not just *we* that counts.

Alex: Don't I know it.

Julia: What does that mean?

Alex: Well, Julia, your opinion is always the one that, ultimately, counts.

Julia: I pay the bills. It's my house.

Alex: That's a really cheap shot. That is beneath you, Julia. I contribute my fair whack. I'm on thirty-five grand a year, now.

Julia: I know. I'm sorry. I'm just angry with Kate.

Alex: Fucking Kate. I suppose, moving in with her mother is not the ideal way to eradicate an ex from your life, is it?

Julia: No. I'll have a shot of that whisky, please. Have you got a glass?

Alex: You don't, generally, drink whisky.

Julia: I fancy one.

Alex grudgingly walks downstairs to fetch another glass, returns to bed and pours two fingers of whisky for Julia.

Julia: How has work been this week? Did you get the Virgin account? You never talk about work anymore.

Alex: Didn't get it. Working on a new site for Jaffa Cakes.

Julia: Ah. Jaffa Cakes. Who are you working on it with?

Alex: No-one. Well, same old. The usual team.

Julia: Bob? Tim?

Alex: Yeah. God, can we not talk about work Julia? D'you mind if I finish watching this video?

Julia: Fine.

Julia can't quite put her finger on it, but something feels wrong...

2

ALEX AT WORK

he sun cascades down through the high Victorian skylights above his head, casting pools of light on the entrance area to the office. At the hot-desking area where Alex sits, just beyond reception, it is cool and shady.

A tall, slim blonde woman glides through the double doors from the landing beyond, propelled on high stilettos, a delicate white chiffon skirt shuddering around her thighs as she moves. She has a long, aquiline face, slim nose, full lips and bright, inquisitive blue eyes; she is stunning.

She stops in the sunlight and examines one of her fingernails, then sucks it, thoughtfully. Aware that she's being watched, she quickly shakes her shoulder-length wavy hair, then resumes walking towards Alex.

❧❧❧

She's...what's the word...she's actually *sashaying*. How does she *do* that? No-one else on earth walks like that. She actually *slides through the air*. And that grin when she sees me. Does she fancy me? Hard to tell. She gets on with everybody.

Sandi: Hi, sweets.
Alex: Long lunch hour.

Sandi: Haven't even *had* lunch. I was in a meeting with that prat from accounts, Julian. God he's tedious. I nearly fell asleep three times. My head was actually nodding, you know, when you suddenly jolt awake?

Alex: Julian, can't place him.

Sandi: The one from *Birmingham*.

Alex: Oh, him.

See? Look at that...the way she's looking into my eyes and smiling at me.

Sandi: How did you get on with the content in the left hand sidebar?

Alex: I've rewritten it. Have a look.

I can smell her. It's not even perfume, it's just her. That floaty white outfit she wears, she looks like an angel. Oh for fuck's sake Alex shut up.

Sandi: Ha! Got it! It pops! Nice one Alex!

She's looking at me again as she sits down on the adjacent stool, opening her laptop onto the shared desk area.

Sandi: What is it? God you've been looking miserable for days, Alex. Is something wrong?

Alex: What, me? No. Course not.

Sandi: Go on. I can tell. I've been working on the Jaffa Cake account with you for weeks now, I can read your moods.

Alex: You can?

Sandi: I can, Alex, I can.

Alex: How?

She's got her iPhone out now and is fiddling with the soft gel case, whilst glancing up at me occasionally.

Sandi: Well, to be honest, it's pretty obvious. You just don't seem happy. Well, you're alright here at work. But every day when you arrive, you've got this hang-dog expression on your face, as though you've got the weight of the world on you. Then it returns just before you leave the office.

Alex: Maybe I *have* got the weight of the world on me.

Sandi: I thought you said nothing was wrong?

I'm not aware that I just let out a deep sigh. I'm only aware of her fragrance as I breathe in again. I feel giddy with her.

Alex: Well something *is* wrong, OK?

Sandi: Family problems?

Alex: Kind of.

Sandi: What? Tell me.

Alex: God, I already had this conversation not so long ago, in a field of flowers.

Sandi: Alex, only you could sound romantic when you're pouring your heart out. What do you mean?

Alex: I'd gone to help my mother-in-law after her car broke down. I ended up telling her what a mess my relationship with her daughter was in, i.e. my wife. And...and we fell in love. Right there and then. In the field. It just happened.

Sandi: You fell in love...hold on...let me get this right...you fell in love with your *mother-in-law?*

Alex: Bingo.

Sandi: I've seen her photo...on your screensaver...I mean it's obvious she's a lot older than you...what...about thirty years older?

Alex: Twenty-six...

Sandi: Right. So...it's a mess then?

Alex: She gets frustrated with me. Because of the age gap. She's...mellow. She doesn't laugh out loud at anything before half a bottle of Pinot. She's...not boring...she's interesting...she's a writer...but we just don't have the same sense of humour. I feel old before my time.

Sandi: Alex! Oh, I'm so sorry. You poor thing...

Alex: She's lovely. She's beautiful...

Sandi: I can tell. From her photos. Probably really slim when she was younger as well.

Alex: She was. Look, she's middle-aged.

Sandi: Of course, I'm sure. Yes. Quite.

Alex: I think I'm bored. I think we're both bored. I never thought I'd say that. We couldn't keep our hands off one another when we got together.

Sandi: Do you still...do you...have a sex life? Or is she...well... they go off it, don't they? Older women...you know...they *dry up*. Kind of. Not meaning. Not in a bad way. If you know what I mean.

Alex: We still have sex, yes.

Sandi: So when was the last time? I mean, you sound as though it's a problem. And I'm here to listen, Alex, you know that. And it's confidential of course.

Alex: Last night.

Is that my imagination or did a cloud of disappointment just pass over Sandi's otherwise perfectly manicured face? Her bottom lip, glossy with pink lipstick, is almost pouting. Was that a flash of sadness? She's gazing into my eyes. God, now I've got an erection. Fucking typical.

Sandi: Oh, I see. Last night. So your sex life isn't *that* spasmodic, then.

Alex: I still find her attractive, Sandi. She *is* attractive. And I love her. I just don't think I'm *in love* with her anymore. And I'm fed up with the way she talks to me.

Sandi: How does she talk to you?

Alex: Patronising. As though I'm a kid. I'm thirty-one years old! It's not like I'm sixteen or something.

Sandi: Quite. You could, technically, be a grand-parent at thirty-two.

Alex: And bossy. She *mothers me.* It never used to bother me. But it has, lately.

⅌⅌⅌

He is gorgeous. Fuck, I wish he weren't living with that old prune, Julia. What a waste. I love his brown eyes. His curly hair. His clothes. Smart, you could take him anywhere, but he's not an *urbanite.* He's like, country casual. He wears these green corduroys and these brogues. Not fashionable at all, but *so* fucking gorgeous. He's wearing them now. *That* is a bulge in his pants. *Fuck!* He's got a hard-on! *Talking to me!*

Sandi: Well, Alex, you know what I think. Life if short. If it's not working, end it. Just move out. You're not married, are you? No kids? Well, she's got kids, one of them being *your ex-wife!*

Alex: One kid. Just Kate. No more.

Sandi: Well, it's up to you. But you're young. You're wasting your youth. Fuck, Alex, she's going to be...if she's twenty-six years older...she'll be *seventy* in *thirteen years. That* is an *old lady.*

Alex: You're doing a great job of trying to persuade me to keep this going, Sandi.

Even when he blinks, he's gorgeous. His eyelashes are gorgeous. I want to touch them. I want to touch him. I want to open his shirt and touch his chest. I want to unbutton his corduroys and see his cock. Oh, god, I want him so much.

Sandi: I'm just being honest, Alex. You asked for my opinion. I'd be doing you a disservice as a friend if I lied to you, wouldn't I? You don't just want some kind of yes-man as a friend, do you?

Alex: I didn't know we were friends. I like that.

Sandi: You don't think I talk to everyone at work like this, do you?

Alex: You seem to get on with everyone...

Sandi: That's different. *You're* different.

Alex: I...we...we'd better crack on.

We had, Alex. We'd better 'crack on' as you say, otherwise I'm going to melt into a puddle from the heat of you.

3
MATT AND KATE

hy does she read this shite? Grazia magazine. She's flicking through the pages, smiling to herself every now and then enunciating sharp, pithy little phrases of condemnation.

'She fucking well deserves it! Look at the state of her!' and 'What a nightmare.' and the simple, straightforward, all-encompassing 'Bitch!'

Eighteen months living together, the longest I've ever lived with anyone, although we hardly ever see one another. My modelling career ('career', what a joke, it probably won't last another five years) takes me abroad for weeks at a time and when I'm at home there are always little projects which keep Kate and I apart.

Installing a new central heating system and then putting an en-suite bathroom in for Kate took weeks of my spare time. We could have paid someone but I love plumbing, me. It dun't pretend, it dun't answer back and it dun't bitch. It's therapy.

She's wearing a little yellow cotton vest, Stella McCartney. Her nipples are protruding through the fabric, small, sweet, stiff. I see nipples all the time at work and somehow they mean nowt. But Kate does summat to me. She can be a mercurial little viper, but the packaging is gorgeous. Five foot three, shoulder-length brown bobbed hair, sweet little face and fire in her amber eyes. Do I love her? No idea. I'm fond of her. It's nice coming home to her clothes strewn everywhere, her silly magazines, empty packets of Marks and Spencers salads strewn over the work-surfaces. It's company I suppose and I can't be arsed to do owt to change the status quo.

❧❧❧

God, Ryan Gosling's hot. Hmmm. Looks better in the jeans than the shorts. I like the shorts. I'd give anything to fuck Ryan Gosling. I should just go to LA and hang out there and hope I bump into him, he'd be bound to fancy me. Maybe I shouldn't be thinking like this. Fuck it. I'm allowed to lech over other men. Fuck me, I bet Matt spends most of his time leching over those scarecrows he works with. I bet he fucks them, too, I wouldn't put it past him. Tall, perfect body, blonde curly hair, lovely nose, brown eyes. He's the perfect looking bloke really. In fact, I've done really well, first Alex who was gorgeous and now Matt who's a top model. Alex was a boring twat though, doesn't make up for good looks. At least Matt's interesting. And away a lot, so I'm free most of the time. Perfect, really.

❧❧❧

Kate: Why are you staring at my nipples?

Matt: Dunt yer want me to look at yer nah, then? Yer 'ot Katie-watie, that's why ah look at yer!

Kate: I'm just hot am I? That's all there is to me, is it?

Matt: Nah, yer can make good Yorkshire Puds too.

Kate: Very funny. When was the last time I made them? They're Northerners' food. I don't care how many trendy restaurants are doing bangers and mash and Yorkshire fucking Puddings, I still consider it food that peasants eat.

Matt: Oh ah see. We're all peasants nah is it?

Kate: Well, not all of you. I don't think Sean Bean's a peasant. He was lovely in *Game of Thrones*. He's cultured, see? I bet he goes to the opera, Sean Bean.

Matt: He goes to t' footy. Blades supporter.

Kate: He's into football? How uncouth. I've gone right off him.

Matt: He's allas there when he's in t'UK. Passionate, he is. A passion for footie. Like ah've gorra passion for classic cars, that sort o' thing.

Kate: How fascinating. Like I said, I've gone off him now.

Matt: Yer like Ryan Gosling though, ah can see...

Kate: There's a good story about him in Grazia, that's all.

Matt: Well, when yer've finished reading that shite, 'appen yer'd like me to fuck yer Katie.

Kate: I would, actually.

❦❦❦

Kate pulls her vest over her head revealing her small, pert breasts with stiff, dark nipples pointing slightly upwards. Matt is already hard, his penis is swollen to its full size and is sticking upright making a tent in the sheet. He pulls the sheet off him, looks down at his cock then gently strokes the length of the shaft with his forefinger. Kate leans over and brushes the tip of her right nipple against his hairless chest and runs her finger around his nipple. Matt looks at her then pulls her towards him and kisses her deeply. She wraps a slender leg around his hips and grinds her pelvis into his thigh. Already he can feel that her pussy is moist as she rubs against him. She pulls away from the kiss and moves down the bed towards his cock and trails her tongue up the shaft, lightly stroking his penis with her fingers as she does so. She pulls the foreskin back revealing the taut, pink, shiny head of his cock and pushes her lips against it, parting them and engulfing the whole head in her warm mouth.

Matt sighs with pleasure and runs his fingers through her hair. Now she pushes her mouth all the way down the length of his penis, encasing it until it reaches her throat, sucking deeply on it and sucking all the way up it again until the head emerges again from her moist lips. She caresses all around it with her tongue, gently licking, teasing, sucking, before engulfing his entire penis in her mouth once again. When the head of his cock emerges again she licks all around it and sucks the pink, bulbous head gently.

She's feeling unbearably aroused now and slips her right hand between her legs and caresses her pussy, sliding her middle finger down into its silky folds where she rubs her clitoris with quick, delicate strokes. She rests her elbows on Matt's thighs as her head moves up and down, up and down, rhythmically pumping his cock with her warm, soft mouth and moist tongue, causing waves of velvet electricity to surge up and down Matt's body. He wants to shoot inside her right now but also wants to fuck her so holds back his orgasm.

Kate is wiggling her bottom as she masturbates, grinding her crotch into the sheets as her finger flicks back and forth over her clitoris. She starts breathing heavily as she sucks the head of Matt's penis and has to withdraw her mouth to catch her breath.

The engorged head of his cock is almost purple now and stretched taut. Kate breathes more and more heavily as she flicks her little tongue out to catch the pearlescent blobs of pre-come oozing from the slit at the end of his cock. The salty smooth liquid almost drives her mad with ecstasy and she starts coming, moaning and gasping as her hips grind her pussy into the bedding.

Before she has a chance to recover she slides up Matt's body, sits astride him and impales herself on his stiff penis, which prises apart the lips of her vulva and slides into the depths of her wet, oily pussy. He gasps and wraps his hands around her hips. She is so slim and lithe that he pulls her into him and lifts her off him effortlessly. Every time the full length of his cock is inside her, she wiggles her hips, moving his penis inside her for a few seconds before he pulls her off him again and then plunges her back down, encasing his cock in the hot, wet folds of her pussy.

Matt can feel the tide of his approaching orgasm about to wash over him. He removes his hands up from Kate's hips and cups her breasts in his hands, rubbing his palms over her erect nipples, awash and delirious with the feel of her firm breasts under his fingers, tweaking her nipples which point so gracefully upwards. She gasps with pleasure, takes control and rides him as he thrusts in and out of her, pounding his cock into the moist depths of her pussy. With one final thrust he throws his hands down and grabs her pert little bottom, pulling her into him, keeping her there, his penis deep inside her as he spurts long jets of semen deep inside her, his mind and body exploding together into a throbbing storm of pleasure. Simultaneously, Kate cries out and with her hips keeps grinding herself into his cock as he comes.

Kate flops down onto him and sighs, kisses his chest then rolls off him and curls into his side. Matt sighs heavily with deep pleasure.

Matt: Katie-watie. Still a fantastic fuck.
Kate: So are you. The best ever.

After a couple of minutes of silence, they start talking again.

Matt: Ah'd still like to meet 'im, yer know. Yer ex. Alex.
Kate: I hate him. And I pretty much still hate my mother. So it would be...awkward.

Matt: Ah know luv. But it's yer mam. We've been together all this time and ah've still not met yer mam! It's not reyt!

Kate: My 'mam' stole my husband, Matt!

Matt: Well, not really, luv. Ah mean, you were shagging that tosser Colin. So you weren't bein' faithful in t' first place were yer?

Kate: That's not the point. The point is that you are not meant to fuck your mother-in-law. It's unnatural. It's...it's...incest!

Matt: It ain't Katie. It ain't incest. They're not related, like, are they?

Kate: Whatever. She shouldn't have done it. And the thought he's now living in my childhood home. Having sex with my mother! It's just fucking disgusting. Unnatural.

Matt: Why don't you let me judge for mesen? I mean it Kate, I think it's time ah met her. We could invite her round for tea or summat.

Kate: I'm not ready, Matt. Not now. Not yet...

Matt: Well, I want to meet her. At some point. Soon, OK?

4

COLIN AND SANDI AT THE LOOPHOLE OPENING

he audacious Victorian baroque building housing The South London Art Gallery, colloquially known as SLAG, stands dramatic and timeless in the late afternoon spring sunlight.

Inside is the Creative Lounge, housed in a double-height room and lit with wide skylights. Loophole, the documentary film company, are having a wine and canapés opening for their new cross-platform division, hosted by the charismatic young Chinese entrepreneur, Dan Bong.

The full-height patio doors are open onto the Fox Garden and the upper walls are shining with the now famous Paul Morrison gold-leaf mural. Anyone who is anyone on the London media scene will be here.

Colin Farmer is one of the first to arrive. Medium height, long nose, thin lips and wide, startled eyes, he looks like he's permanently on coke. Although in his late thirties, he's sporting the swept-forward mop-top haircut popular with seventeen year olds. Tonight, Colin is dressed in skinny-fit Calvin Klein jeans, white Calvin Klein t-shirt and black leather ankle boots. All he's carrying is an iPhone.

He pauses by the reception desk at the room entrance. The young arty-looking girl with a large whirl of blond bun either side of her head, smiles warmly at him.

Arty-looking buns girl: Good evening. Name, please?

Colin glances at the guest list in front of the girl. She holds a marker pen in mid-air, waiting patiently.

Colin: Farmer.

Arty-looking buns girl: And your first name please?

Colin: There will only be one of me.

Arty-looking buns girl: There are two, actually. Helen or Colin?

Colin: Hilarious babes. Co.Lin. Obviously.

The girl hands him a little blue raffle ticket.

Arty-looking buns girl: This entitles you to one free drink. Have a lovely evening.

Colin takes the ticket and looks away immediately, before wandering into the room.

Long high tables line the perimeter of the room, each one with several stools in front of it, the hot-desking area. The centre of the room is clear apart from a long makeshift bar near the windows, where a young lad wearing thick-rimmed black spectacles is methodically polishing glasses, his little moustache twitching as he wrinkles his nose up at any trace of dirt.

Colin grabs a glass of white wine from the table and ignores the lad then looks around him as slowly, the room starts to fill up. Within half an hour, the place is teeming with suits and fashionistas.

Uncomfortable that he can't see a familiar face, Colin finally spots someone he knows at the other side of the room. What's her name again? He remembers her from a Christmas do a few months back. She's wearing a short, flirty skirt in lemon chiffon, white platform stilettos and a white lace blouse, unbuttoned slightly to reveal a pink lacy bra. That's her alright. Legs up to her tits. Colin wouldn't forget a body like that in a hurry. He marches over to her, purposefully, holding up his glass of wine.

Colin: My good friends Mr Pinot and Mr Grigio appear to be absent this evening. Only this lukewarm shit.

Sandi: Oh...

Colin: I remember the face. Beauty like that is unforgettable. Can't quite remember your name, though.

Sandi: It's Sandi. Have we met before?

Colin: At the Saatchi Christmas do. Don't you remember? You spilt wine over yourself.

Sandi: You spilt wine over me. Yes, how could I forget.

Colin: Well, lovely to see you again. You've cleaned yourself up, I see.

Sandi: What do you mean?

Colin: After the spillage. Had a wash. Changed your clothes.

Sandi: It was *months* ago.

Colin: Only jesting with you. So, know many people here?

Sandi: Lots. I was just on my way to join some of them.

Colin: You were looking lost and lonely you mean.

Sandi: I wasn't.

Colin: Babes, you were. I know a woman who's in need of company. I can smell them a mile off.

Sandi: I'm not in need of company. And you can't smell me.

Colin: I can, actually. Gorgeous perfume. What is it?

Sandi: Dior.

Colin: Yeah but *which one?*

Sandi: It's Dior Addict Eau Fraich if you must know.

Colin: Classy.

Sandi: I should go.

Colin: You work at Bates & Bartle, don't you?

Sandi: How on earth do you know that?

Colin: Because you were with some other people I know from there. Tim Donaghey? Bob Joakim?

Sandi: I was, yes. How do you know them?

Colin: We've used them before. I'm at Ogilvy and Mather. Won a Gold Lion for my Munch Bunch campaign.

Sandi: A Gold Lion?

Colin: Cannes, sweetie. The fucking Palme D'Or of advertising, yeah?

Sandi: Really. So...you know Jim Franklin then?

Colin: Jim and I, we go back years, course I do babes.

Sandi: Would you do me a big favour, Colin?

Colin: Name it. I'm there.

Sandi: Would you stop calling me 'Babes'? It wasn't funny at the turn of the millennium and it certainly isn't funny now.

Colin: This isn't about humour, babes. I'm abso-fucking-lutely serious. You are the most gorgeous bird in here.

Sandi: Right. So, you're single. You're not married? With kids, or anything?

Colin: Kids? You have got to be kidding. *Kidooks?* I can't be tied down by kids. Too many demands.

Sandi: And a wife? A girlfriend?

Colin: You sound interested.

Sandi: I'm not.

Colin: Well, cool it with the questions, babes. I'm a free man, believe me.

Sandi: Strangely enough, I don't find that concept very far-fetched. I just don't want your wife storming over to cause a scene because your hand is moving very close to my arse and I'd like you to move it away, please.

Colin: No wives. No ex-wives. No woman's ever managed to tame me.

Sandi: Really. So, you're wild, like an untamed lion?

Colin: Not a word I like to use, 'lion'. Too cuddly. 'Furry' almost. I'd like to describe myself as more like an...an eagle. Soaring over the plains. Free.

Sandi: And on the hunt for prey. I see. Anyway. It's been lovely talking to you but I have to go and join my friends.

Colin: Before you go. I've got a table booked at Sashimi Grove for this Thursday. Business. Colleague had to fly out to our Hong Kong agency at the last minute. Cancelled. Fancy joining me?

Sandi: Sashimi Grove?

Colin: Yeah. *The* Sashimi Grove. Japanese. Where all the celebs go.

Sandi: Sashimi Grove may be fashionable, Colin, but have you ever seen The Sashimi Grove cookbook?

Colin: Not my usual reading material, no.

Sandi: Apart from *Nuts*, you mean.

Colin: And the *Financial Times*.

Sandi: Naturally. Well, in the Sashimi Grove cookbook are instructions on how to cut the beak from a live octopus and then turn its head inside out. Whilst it's still alive. It is, quite frankly, disgusting.

Colin: You're not one of them *freaks* are you, babes? A *vegan?*

Sandi: No. But I think cutting parts off a live animal is...it's just...unforgiveable. If people knew what went on in the kitchens they wouldn't eat there. Anyway, look, I must go.

Colin: So, that's a 'no' then. We could go to Kentucky Fried Chicken in Notting Hill Gate if you want.

Sandi: Colin, I really hate to be rude...

Colin: Nah, it's fine babes. I've wasted enough time as it is. Got people to talk to, can't stand here all evening.

Sandi: Lovely. Bye then.

Sandi stands watching Colin's receding figure and can't quite believe what she's just been part of. Do men like that really still exist? Obviously they do. Was he taking the piss? Judging by his haircut, no, he's absolutely serious. How the fuck he's an art director at a prestigious agency like Ogilvy and Mather is completely beyond her.

Sean McAllister, the documentary filmmaker whose website Sandi built the year before, approaches her. Medium height, cropped, salt and pepper hair and a cheeky, impudent grin with glittering green eyes full of mischief. Thank fuck. Somebody she actually likes.

Sandi: Sean!

Sean: Sandi! How are you?

Sandi: Fine! How are you? Rough time over in Syria with your documentary, I heard?

Sean: Eventful, yeah. No cunt will commission it and I've been back thirteen times now. Who was that bloke you were talking to?

Sandi: He's called Colin something and he is the biggest fucking tosser I think I've ever met.

Sean: He looked like he was about to grope your arse, Sandi.

Sandi: He was, and he would have got a slap.

Sean: From me. Wanker.

Sandi: Cunt, actually. You know you end up talking to someone sometimes and they are so awful that you carry on talking to them because you can't quite believe what utter wankers they are?

Sean: Yeah...

Sandi: Like that. I really hope I never run into him again.

Dan Bong from Shine walks up to Sandi and Sean and puts a friendly hand on each of their shoulders.

Dan: Enjoying it? I hope so! There was only meant to be 100 on the guest list and I've got 130! Hope it doesn't get too rammed! Hey Sandi...the guy who was talking to you then...are you OK? He wasn't bothering you?

Sandi. Nah, it's fine.

Dan: He's a big wheel...got to be nice to him...part of the job... hard sometimes. I wish everyone were like you and Sean here.

Sandi: So do I. Well, I probably won't see him again for a long time, if ever. Ship in the night. Hallelujia.

Sean holds his glass up and grins.

Sean: Amen. Cheers!

5

THE MATTHEW WILLIAMSON AFTER-SHOW PARTY

ate's best friend, Tanya, dangles her legs from the stool she's sitting on at the bar in the BFI cafe on the South Bank. Tall, with long, layered brunette hair and fashionably thick-rimmed spectacles, her lips pouting with red lipstick, she sips languidly on an iced green tea. She's wearing denim shorts, flat sneakers and a floaty floral blouse. Her legs are unfeasibly long; wasted as a PA to a haulage contractor, she could have been a model, and she knows it.

Tanya: There is absolutely no fucker here.

Kate: I know. It's usually teeming with gorgeous blokes.

Tanya: Only one reservation. Sick of fucking beards.

Kate: Me too. Makes them look old.

Tanya: Where do blokes get off thinking beards are attractive, anyway? They're vile. They tickle when you kiss.

Kate: Hate them, babes.

Tanya: I know. We have this conversation at least once a week.

Kate: Intellectuals, that's us.

Tanya: I s'pose they think it makes them look like screenwriters or something.

Kate: It doesn't. It makes them look stupid. If Matt grew a beard I'd tell him to get rid of it.

Tanya: Jelz. Matt is fucking hot.

Kate: Yeah. He is...yeah...I guess...

Tanya: What?

Kate: I can't put my finger on it. We're meant to be madly in love.

Tanya: And you're not...

Kate: Well, what you do you think? Do you think we come across as a couple who are madly in love?

Tanya: Don't see you together often enough.

Kate: Well that's coz he never wants to go where I want to go. I mean, I can't believe it. He's a top model for fuck's sake. Have you seen him on the H&M posters down the tube?

Tanya: I haven't actually.

Tanya pointedly looks out and across at her racing bike, attached to the railings just outside the cafe by the Thames.

Kate: What?

Tanya: My bike. Bradley Wiggins. Tour de France. Me.

Kate: Oh yeah. Well, the H&M campaign is everywhere.

Tanya: Ooooh *the campaign* now is it?

Kate: Well...yeah...but you know I never see any *benefit*. OK the money's good, we can eat out whenever we like, it's not like when I was with Alex. But I thought it would be a bit more *glamorous*. You know, living with a *top model*.

Tanya: But *babes, it is!* We've got invites to Matthew Williamson's *after-show party* at the fucking fuck-off fuckadoodle-dandy *Tate Modern!*

Kate: I know. That is great. I'm really looking forward to that.

Tanya: See? We wouldn't be going if it weren't for Matt, eh?

Kate: Phwoar. Look at *him*.

A bloke in his late twenties has just sat down on the terrace, alone. He's got short, dark, wavy hair, a thick, bushy beard and is wearing Ray-Ban aviators in metallic blue. He plonks a large cup of coffee on the table in front of him, whips out a laptop, fires it up and then hunches over it, typing furiously.

Tanya: A *writer*.

Kate: A *screenwriter*.

Tanya: I need to know who he is. He's *got* to be someone. He *has* to be.

Kate: Talk to him. Go on, ask him who he is.

Tanya: Don't be stupid, Kate.

Kate: I will, then.

Tanya: He's got a beard...

Kate: There is that. He's gorgeous though.

Tanya: It's a nice idea. If I had the time, I would. Saunter over to him. Chat him up. But I don't. I've got to be going, I've got the dentist's at four.

Kate: Me too. I've actually promised to cook tonight. Matt wants Yorkshire Pudding, bangers and mash.

Tanya: How *suburban*.

Kate: I know.

Kate idly picks up her mobile phone and checks her messages. The two sit in silence for several minutes, whilst Tanya tries not to look at the bloke with the beard. Eventually Kate puts her phone down on the table and sighs, heavily.

Kate: It's not like I don't love Matt...it's just...anyway...we'd better go.

Tanya: I know.

Kate and Tanya pick up their bags and exit through the French windows leading out onto the late afternoon-sunlit terrace. As they walk past the bloke with the beard, Kate drops her keys onto the floor. They land with a clatter on the ground, but the bloke with the beard carries on typing, his fingers flying over the keyboard as he types another page of the pet project he's working on, 'How I Learnt to Understand Women.'

Kate: Oh! I dropped my keys!
Tanya: Oh, Kate! Where are they?

Kate is standing only a couple of feet away from the bloke with the beard. As Tanya scoops to the floor to retrieve the keys, Kate grins a disarmingly wide and beautiful smile at the bloke, tilting her head slightly so that her hair swings over her face. He glances up at her, completely ignores her, looks back down and carries on typing. Kate and Tanya walk towards Tanya's parked bike.

Kate: Wanker.
Tanya: Arsehole. Men with beards, I told you.
Kate: He's not a man, he's a boy.
Tanya: Pathetic.
Kate: Pearls before swine. Did you see the way he looked at me?
Tanya: No. I was picking up your keys. How did he look at you?
Kate: Like a wanker.
Tanya: Coz he is.

Tanya unlocks and mounts her bike, kisses Kate goodbye and cycles off into the distance. Kate walks away into the afternoon sunshine, her shoulders slightly hunched, swinging her clutch bag. The bloke with the beard stops typing and stares after them both, his lips slightly parted, his heart suddenly beating fast as he watches Tanya slip out of his life.

༂ར་༂ར་༂ར

Kate: I'm sorry. I know they've not risen properly.

Matt: It's fine Katie-watey. Don't worry about it. They're grand, luv.

Kate: No they're not, they're rubbish Yorkshire Puddings.

Matt: Not as good as me mam makes, no, but yer'v got competition there.

Kate: Just what I wanted to hear when I've bothered to spend my afternoon off slaving over a hot stove for you.

Matt: You've been cooking all afternoon?

Kate: No, actually. I went up to London to meet Tanya.

Matt: Oh reyt. Where did ya go?

Kate: BFI cafe.

Matt: Any good?

Kate: Full of wankers with beards. Being wankers.

Matt: What, ignoring yer?

Kate: Something like that. *No!* Not ignoring me. Not paying attention, not anything! Just...*posing!* I'm so sick of fucking *posers!*

Matt: Well I'd have soon as gone for a pint down the King's Arms.

Kate: *No-one* goes there.

Matt: What do you mean *no-one?*

Kate: No-one *interesting.*

Matt: *I* go there. Dunt yer find me interesting anymore? Is that it, Kate?

Kate: Oh for fuck's sake. You know what I mean.

Matt: I don't know what you mean actually. What qualifies someone as uninteresting?

Kate: Office types.

Matt: Like you and Tanya.

Kate: That is just bitchy, Matt. Why do you have to turn everything into a row, nowadays?

Matt: Love, I'm not. I'm just trying to 'ave a conversation. Find out what yer mean by interesting or uninteresting.

Kate: Writers, artists, media types, filmmakers. You know, *interesting.*

Matt: Well that's a laff for a start. Since when were you arsed about literature and art house films?

Kate: You're trying to twist my words! You're trying to corner me!

Matt: I'm not, Kate, I'm trying to find out what makes yer tick, because even after eighteen months I've got no fuckin' idea, luv. I mean, art, artists, since when you were interested in art?

Kate: I'm very interested in art I'll have you know!

Matt: Well, that's good to hear Kate, that's good to hear. Because...

Kate: What?

Matt: Well...because...there's been a change of plan...

Kate: What do you mean?

Matt: The Matthew Williamson after-show party. I'm not going.

Kate: You *what?*

Matt: I'm not going, luv. It clashes with the opening night of the new exhibition at the National Portrait Gallery.

Kate: What new fucking exhibition?

Matt: *First Exposure.*

Kate: What's that?

Matt: Iconic photographs from the sixties till now. There's five of Jimmy Page. Really want to see them.

Kate: Well you can go and see them any time Matt! This is fucking Matthew Williamson's after-show party!

Matt: And it'll be full of knobs from work and people wanting to talk to me. I can't be arsed, Kate. I'd rather go to the NPG.

Kate: I don't fucking *believe* this!

Matt: There's everything that there'll be at Matt's do. Wine and canapés, the usual.

Kate: Yes, wine and fucking canapés, yes, but the wrong fucking *people!* It's not all about *fucking wine and fucking canapés!*

Matt: It's not *even* about them, Kate. It's about the *photographs.* The *work.* The *art.* You just said, for fuck's sake, that you want to mix with the right people i.e. artists! What the fuck's wrong with you?

Kate: Because, Matt, *Tatler* will not be covering some stupid photos at some *stupid art gallery*, that's why. Tatler will be at fucking *Matthew Williamson's!*

Matt: So that's it, is it? You just want to get yersen in some crappy rag like *Tatler?*

Kate: *Tatler* is not *crappy.* It's a guide as to *who's in* and *who's out.*

Matt: I wouldn't wipe me arse on it.

Kate: Well you're a *snob*, then. You're just being *elitist.*

Matt: Ya know full well that one thing ah'm *not* is a *snob*, so yer can *pack that in* fer a start, luv. Look. You can go to Matt's do with Tanya, can't you? I don't need to go.

Kate: But it won't be the same without you! No one knows who I am!

Matt: So yer *need* me there.

Kate: Well, actually, *yes I do!* Me and Tanya! We *both do!*

Matt: Fer what, exactly? Fer attention? So people think yer fuckin' great coz yer with Matthew Dent, the top model? Is that it Kate? Is that all I fucking am to yer? *Someone to be seen with?* Eh?

Kate: You're doing it again. Typical! Twisting my words! You *Northerners*, you're all the same. You pride yourselves on being 'straight oop' but you're devious! Nothing's ever *clear* with you, is it? *Is it*, Matt?

Matt: Yer know what? Yer can be a spiteful little gob-shite when yer fancy it. Yer can go to Matt's do with Tanya. Ah'm goin' to t'exhibition openin' and that's fucking *that*.

6

TANYA AND THE BLOKE WITH THE BEARD AT THE BFI CAFE

ate is jabbering on. The sun looks warm outside on the empty terrace filled with chairs, but we're sitting in here, in the cool, dark depths of the bar, illuminated only by the green lighting recessed in the ceiling, casting an eerie glow on the expanse of sparkling quartz beneath.

The sounds of the river boats on the Thames just beyond the terrace, distant traffic and birdsong from the trees float in from outside and join the sounds of in here; a low hum from the air-conditioning and the waitress clattering behind the bar and refilling her coffee machine which hisses, churns and spits.

A bloke walks past me and up to the bar, he's wearing stone-coloured chinos, Birkenstock sandals and a vintage cheesecloth long sleeve shirt. He's got dark hair down to just below his ears, wavy, nicely styled, and a full, brown beard. He's wearing metallic blue aviators, Ray-Bans, pushed up onto his head. He glances at me as he waits to order. His eyes are like some kind of fern green or something, really beautiful. He's got really long eyelashes. He looks away again.

The waitress behind the bar takes his order. He asks for an espresso. His voice is really deep. He has a London accent, slightly posh. I shift in my seat, uncross my legs, and stretch one of them out in front of me, wiggling my foot in the air. I've painted my toenails gold and they're sparkling greeny-gold in the lights from the bar. He doesn't seem to notice. The waitress slowly slides his espresso across the bar. He looks up at her and smiles. His smile is gorgeous, warm, tender, slow.

He picks his coffee up and turns, glancing across at me once again. The smile has faded from his face, he looks me straight in the eye, catches my gaze and my heart lurches.

He walks outside and the sun bleaches him for a second before he sits down under the canopy at a table straight in front of us, maybe twenty feet away. He places his coffee on the table in front of him and pulls a laptop from a brown, leather satchel. He opens it up and waits for it to boot up. Then he takes a sip of coffee, puts the coffee down, and starts typing.

I am mesmerised by him. Kate's voice has slipped into the distance, out of earshot and her face is blurred. I slide off the stool and walk away from her and towards the man with the beard. I'm wearing a short chiffon dress which buttons down the front and barely covers my bottom. My legs are tanned and I'm wearing stilettos. I walk towards him slowly, the dress swishing gently against my thighs, and then stop right by him, looking down at him.

He stops typing. I can see what he's writing on the screen...

'Her legs are tanned. She's wearing stilettos. She walks towards me slowly, her dress swishing gently against her thighs, and then stops right by me, looking down at me. I want to unbutton her dress and caress her breasts, slide my hands inside her knickers, hold her bottom, push my fingers into her pussy, lift her onto the table and fuck her.'

I sit down on the chair, next to him.

He looks into my eyes. He reaches over and cups his hand behind my neck, pulls me towards him and kisses me deeply. His mouth is soft and warm, his tongue gentle and probing. The contrast of the wiry bush of his beard giving way to the soft moistness of his lips excites me. He kisses me more and more deeply, drawing me towards him, wrapping his other arm around me.

My pussy is aching. I have never wanted a man as much in my life as this. He draws away and gazes at me; he is intoxicatingly beautiful. Still holding my gaze, he slowly unfastens my dress, button by button, so that the fabric gradually peels open, revealing my breasts beneath, first just the curve of the breast, then a glimpse of brown nipple, then the entire nipple, brown and pointing slightly upwards, then the contour of both firm, large, round breasts.

He peels the fabric completely away from my breasts and looks down at them, before gently running both hands over them, caressing the contour of each breast, running his finger over the nipples, cupping the weight of my breasts in his hands, smoothing his fingers over their warm, firm roundness, then sliding his hand down over my flat stomach as he unbuttons and unpeels the rest of my dress, which slips to the floor.

He moves his chair back from the table and moves it closer to mine. He sits with his legs astride and reaches down and unbuttons his trousers, reaches inside and manoeuvres his cock from its sheath of clothing. It is large and swollen, jutting upwards from the fabric of his trousers, the head round and perfect like a deep pink plum. The tip is oily already, I can see it glistening.

He looks into my eyes and pulls me towards him again, kissing me deeply, running his hands up and down my body until I feel feverish with desire for him. I reach across and touch his penis, caress it, hold it, grasp it, move my hand up and down the length of it, slowly and firmly. He moves his mouth slightly apart from mine and gasps with pleasure.

I stand up and draw the fabric of my silky black camisole knickers aside, revealing my pussy which is covered in a small triangle of close-cropped deep brown hair. I straddle him, place one hand on his neck, and with the other, I hold the fabric of my knickers to one side. My pussy is now burning with desire. I lower myself towards the head of his penis and guide it onto the soft folds of my vulva. I stay still, right there, with the tip of his cock gently pushing against me, and I slowly move my hips in circles to tease him.

I lean down and kiss him deeply on the mouth and he reaches down, holds my bottom and with one firm thrust pulls me down, spearing me with one long, deep thrust of his engorged penis. I throw my arms around his neck. The hair on his neck is soft and curly, I run my fingers around his neck and bury my face into it, nuzzling my nose and mouth into the thick forest of his beard, breathing in his scent, deeply, all the while holding still with the full weight of his erect cock inside me.

His hands are large, each one holds a cheek of my bottom and he gently lifts me up and then pulls me back down again, onto him. He feels enormous and my insides feel distended and aching for him. He grabs my waist, pulls my back towards him, his hands are everywhere as he explores me, holds me and rhythmically moves me up and down.

His eyes are half-closed and his lips slightly parted. I lean over and kiss him. He stops moving, reaches down and slips a finger inside the lips of my pussy, gently moving it around, teasing me, and then grasps the base of his cock, holding it for a second whilst holding my bottom with his other hand, holding me in place, waiting for him to start moving again. I am almost frantic with the desire for him to start fucking me again. Still holding the stiff length of his penis with one hand, with the other on my bottom he slowly pulls me back onto him again and holds me there, his cock buried deep inside me, swollen, still, filling me.

He kisses me so deeply now I feel completely lost in him, his teeth, his tongue, his warm mouth, and his penis penetrating inside me, pulling all the way out as he lifts me off him, then pulling me back down until his cock is completely encased in the soft folds of my pussy again.

Gradually he starts fucking me faster and faster. He pulls away from the kiss to breathe and his breathing becomes heavier and heavier as his stiff penis plunges into me. I can feel it distending and engorging even more as he fucks me, faster and faster. I hold his shoulder to steady myself as he moves me up and down. I look down and can see my breasts bouncing gently against him as he fucks me, the nipples grazing the hair on his chest. His penis plunges into me and my insides are liquid as he slips easily in and out, in and out of my pussy, pounding me onto him with crazed desire.

His orgasm approaches and then he throws his head back and cries out as he comes. The thickness of his cock, the rhythm of him thrusting in and out electrify me and I can feel my body pulsating as I come too, waves of pleasure throbbing up through my pussy and all through my body, his cock producing an almost unquenchable desire as he continues thrusting into me through our orgasm.

His gasps recede, my head droops onto his shoulder, my hands holding his neck, my mouth finding his and kissing him deeply into the dying embers of our orgasm.

A heavenly scent wafts towards me; the combined fragrance of his cock and my pussy. I rest my head on his neck as my breathing subsides and he gently kisses my neck, rubbing one hand all the way down my back, tenderly stroking my hair with his other, lifting my hair away from my face and neck and gazing into my eyes. He tells me I'm beautiful, he sighs deeply, he kisses me once more, his tongue warm and soft, his mouth tender and sensuous.

I have never felt happier or more complete as, embraced by his strong arms, I sit astride him, my pussy warm and wet, his cock still buried deep inside me.

He whispers into my ear that now he can write about me properly, and nuzzles his face into my neck. I love him.

The noise of Kate's phone clattering onto the table brings me back to the moment. She says something about how much she loves Matt, and then it's time to go.

7

AN EVENING WITH HARRY STYLES

actually like when Matt's away. Where has he gone this time? The Caribbean. *Without me.* It's alright for him, isn't it? Fucking off to the frigging *Caribbean.* That's not even what I'd call *work.* It's tossing it off, frolicking around on some beach with photographers arse-licking you. Honestly, it's pathetic, his job. Job? Hah! I could do that. *I* could do that. I could model if I was just a bit taller. He says he has to go to all these auditions. Yeah right. Auditions *my arse.* Prancing around London with all his gay mates. I bet he's shagging them. I bet that's why he never wants to shag me anymore. I mean, once a week? It's fucking pathetic, even more pathetic than *pathetic wanky Alex.* That's it, he's a closet case. God how do I pick them? At least I get time without him, without him criticising me for being shallow or whatever else he thinks I am. Which I'm not. Just because I don't want to read National Geographic. Who wants to read about tribesmen and volcanoes? What relevance has that got to *my life, eh?* He can go fuck himself. Or his bum chums. Wotevs.

Kate makes a 'W' shape with her fingers at the mirror and, as she walks past the bed, sweeps a pair of Matt's jeans onto the floor.

I mean, yes, Colin was probably a mistake, but being grown-ups (unlike Alex, who is behaving like a *complete child*, shacking up with my mother) we have put that behind us. Especially now that Emma has dumped him and he's come to his senses. I mean, let's face it, half the problem with me and Colin, no, in fact ninety per cent of the problem now I come to think of it, was *her*. Emma. She completely changed the way he thought. Yes, I liked her when I met her. But I didn't know then just how much she'd warped his mind, did I? Now, I do. Hindsight is wisdom or whatever they say.

I mean, the few times I've seen him since Emma left, he's been a changed man. A hundred per cent. Considerate, polite, funny, all those qualities that were dulled to the point of invisibility by her bad influence. Just like he's pointed out to me.

It's not like I want to get back with him. We're just mates now. But he's going to make some girl *very* happy. Now he's got the promotion at work and they've made him a partner. And he's bought the Bentley Continental. That is just gorgeous. A blue Bentley Continental. Matt doesn't even have a fucking car. I mean, he's always reading Classic Car magazine. Talking the talk. But it's all bollocks.

Kate slumps down on the sofa just as her mobile rings. She picks it up and looks at the number. Talk of the devil! Colin!

Kate: Colin! Hi!
Colin: Babes!
Kate: (giggling) Whassup?
Colin: Godda party lined up, that's what. I thought as that airhead you're shacking up with has fucked off abroad you might fancy slipping along on my suited and booted arm, darlin'.
Kate: What, tonight?
Colin: Yeah babes, tonight.
Kate: Where?
Colin: Highgate, babes. You'll have to uproot yourself from your little nest out in the sticks of Hemel Hempstead and get on a train.
Kate: Oh. You can't come and pick me up?

Colin: Nah. Over the limit. Been to a leaving do at the agency.

Kate: Oh. OK. So, whose party is it?

Colin: I dunno. Some little pop star types. Boy band. One Direction they're called.

Kate: One Direction? They're massive! What, it's their party?

Colin: The singer's.

Kate: Harry Styles? No *way!* He's *gorgeous!* Colin you are *kidding* aren't you? He's like super famous! He's got *ten million followers on Twitter!*

Colin: Not kidding, no. Him. Harry Styles. His party. Highgate. I'm invited. Plus one, natch.

Kate: How did you get an invite, Colin?

Colin: I know him babes. We did an iTunes campaign for his band, One Direction.

Kate: You didn't tell me about that!

Colin: Well, nah, it was last year, when you and I weren't speaking. You know, when Emma was still around.

Kate: I can't believe it. I'm going to meet *Harry Styles!*

Colin: You sure are, darlin'. Get yer booty down here pronto and we're all set to go.

Kate: *Harry Styles!*

ᘿᘿᘿ

Kate gets off the train at St Pancras. Travellers and commuters push and rush coming and going every which way around her. There's going to be no place to get changed so she's had to travel in what she's wearing, a sparkling, shimmering silver dress which floats around her thighs, hugging her slim body, high silver platforms and a white fur shrug. Her hair is long enough now to wear up and she's got it piled high on her head in a bun. She's never looked this good before and she knows it. This isn't for Matt, nor for stupid Alex, nor for her mate Colin and not even for Harry Styles. This is for her, Kate. Because she's going to a fantastic, exciting party in one of the most fashionable areas of London to meet one of the most famous pop stars in the world!

⁂

'Fucking hell. She looks gorgeous. Why the fuck did I let her go?' Colin thinks to himself as Kate struts down the platform towards him. She slots her ticket into the ticket machine and swishes through the barriers with a big grin on her face.

'Darling!' she says, throwing her arms round Colin and kissing him. 'Babes! Missed you!'

'You look fucking hot, Kate. Fuck. I could fuck you right here. Right over this barrier.'

'Colin! Don't talk like that!' says Kate, giggling.

'Seriously, babes. *Seriously. Look at you!*' Colin stands back from Kate's hug and looks her and up and down. She wiggles her hips, parts her lips and laughs, her eyes shining with happiness.

Colin grabs her hand and pulls her along beside him.

'Got any luggage? Are you going back tonight, babes or what?'

'Well, I was wondering if I could stay at yours. If this goes on late I'll miss the last train home. I mean, stay on the couch or something.'

'No problems. Nada, zilcho problemo. Mi coucho es tu coucho.'

Colin and Kate jump into a cab in the long queue of black cabs snaking around the corner outside the back of St Pancras station.

'2 Church Road, Highgate please, chum.' says Colin.

All the way from St Pancras to Highgate, Colin fiddles with his iPhone. Kate looks out of the window at all the property. The Georgian properties, the thirties blocks of flats, the Victorian terraces, and all the people walking past the properties, the businessmen, the students, the housewives, the scruffy, the trendy, the stern and concerned, and imagines herself working in an Estate Agent's in Hampstead, selling properties like these and going for lunch with other interesting people, ruing the fact that she lives in crappy, boring Hemel Hempstead where nothing ever happens.

'Ha ha, look. I've atted him. Harry Styles.' Colin waves his iPhone in front of Kate's face. On the screen it says 'Lookin 4ward to the party mate @Harry_Styles.'

'Oh, you follow him on Twitter? Does he talk to you?' asks Kate, looking impressed.

'Course he does. All the time. He personally supervised the iTunes campaign. Was in my office every fucking lunchtime at one point. Kept nicking my hoi sin duck wraps. Couldn't get rid of the little fucker.'

'Really? Surely he wouldn't have anything to do with an advertising campaign for his band? I mean, it'd be their record company who dealt with the agencies, surely?'

'You've been out of London too long Kate. You've lost touch. Of course he takes a personal interest. He's not just any old boy band member. He's *Harry fucking Styles.*'

'Right.' says Kate, looking dubious and turning to look out of the window again. She turns back and glances at Colin, suspiciously.

'I didn't think you ate duck any more. I thought you'd turned veggie.'

'*Metaphorical* hoi sin duck wraps. It could have been egg mayonnaise sandwiches, I can't fucking remember. All I remember is he was a greedy little fucker.'

'Well, I'm really looking forward to meeting him.' says Kate, uncertain now of what she's letting herself in for.

The cab draws up in front of a large, double-fronted Georgian house with a white, flat-roofed extension to one side.

'This is it!' announces Colin.

'How do you know?' asks Kate. 'Have you been here before?'

Colin looks flustered. 'Nah, course not. Nah. Must be it though cause the cab's stopped here.'

Colin pays and the pair get out of the cab. The quiet, leafy street is almost somnambulant in the early spring evening. There are no other cars parked nearby and no sound of music coming from the house.

'It doesn't look as though there's a party going on.' says Kate, doubtfully.

Colin walks ahead of Kate and into the open entrance porch which is flanked on either side at the front by tall, white Doric columns. He rings the doorbell. Kate waits, impatiently, shifting her weight from one leg to the other, hardly able to contain a rising tide of excitement tinged with bewilderment and suspicion.

The door opens and a little girl of maybe six stands at the door in a fairy outfit, replete with shimmering wings and a tinsel halo on her head.

'What's your name?' she asks, accusingly.

'Um. Colin.' says Colin, sheepishly.

'Mummy it's Colin!' shrieks the little girl, looking backwards over her shoulder.

An elegant woman in her early fifties sashays towards the front door. She's absolutely gorgeous, one of those women who would never dream of touching Botox, who have beautiful faces because they're beautiful inside and out; whose spirit shines through every pore of their skin, where every tiny wrinkle is a reservoir of laughter.

Her name is Sheena and she's wearing a black, full length Indian gown, embroidered with sequins. Her grey hair is piled in a bun on top of her head, like Kate's. Dazzling diamante earrings dangle from her ears as she walks.

'Darling! Colin! How wonderful to see you again! Didn't think you'd actually make it!' she says, a huge grin spreading across her already luminous face.

'Hi Sheena. Um, this is Kate. A...er...friend of mine.'

'And aren't you just the most gorgeous girl!' exclaims Sheena.

'Thanks' says Kate, slightly crestfallen at the enigmatic woman standing grinning at her.

'Come in, come in, both of you!' says Sheena, ushering them through the long hallway which is lined with modern oil paintings.

She leads them into a vast lounge which spans the entire depth of the house, facing out onto the street at the front and onto a lush green garden spreading out beyond the French windows in the distance. Music is booming from inside the house somewhere. 'Riders on the storrrmmm...' laments Jim Morrison with the thrumming base tones over his voice.

An elderly man with glasses and a shock of grey hair sticking up in all directions, seated on a large Chesterfield sofa, nods a brief acknowledgement in Kate and Colin's direction, then picks up a children's book and resumes reading to the little girl, who throws herself gleefully onto the sofa beside him and another little girl wearing a pixie outfit.

Kate suddenly feels desperately uncomfortable. This is obviously not the party Colin had promised her they were going to.

'Drink, darlings?' asks Sheena, amicably.

'Campari and soda.' says Colin, bluntly. 'She'll have the same.'

'Actually, could I just have a glass of white wine?' asks Kate.

'Prosecco? Will that do sweetheart?' asks Sheena.

'Fine.'

Over by the French windows a group of middle-aged women, standing and holding drinks, are chatting politely in low voices. Justine, an elegant brunette of about sixty is pointing at the garden.

'You think topiary has had it? I think topiary's just coming into its own!...ah, *lavender.*'

'Colin. What the frigging hell is this?' hisses Kate. 'I thought this was going to be an amazing party and it's full of old wankers!'

'Shhhh' hisses Colin back at her. 'It's only just started. These must be some of Harry's rellies or something.

'Rellies?'

'Rel-a-tives.'

'So. It's a family party. I see. So how come Harry invited you then?' says Kate in an accusing tone.

Sheena approaches them with the drinks before Colin has a chance to answer. Kate takes her glass of prosecco and smiles.

'Thanks.'

Sheena tilts her head and looks Colin up and down.

'Do you know, you haven't changed since you were two, Colin, you really haven't. I can picture you in that buggy, Joyce walking you through Highgate village, oh were adorable! Those little curls round your ears! Kate, he had curly hair when he was little. And it was blonde. He was so chubby and cute and Oh! I could just squidge those little cheeks right now!' Sheena mischievously reaches out and pinches one of Colin's cheeks and he recoils, his eyes widening with horror.

'So, you knew him as a baby? asks Kate.

'His mother, Joyce was my best friend. That was quite a while before I had Harry and Amy of course. And then Joyce and I lost touch, as you do. And bumping into Colin the other day, well, it was the first time I'd seen him for years! I thought it would be a lovely opportunity to catch up which is why I invited Colin to my little soiree tonight! I was hoping you'd bring your mother though Colin! Where have you got her hidden?'

'Er...she's on holiday.'

'So, *Harry* didn't invite you then Colin?' asks Kate, anger rising inside her.

'I don't think Harry's ever met Colin.' says Sheena, a thoughtful look passing across her face. 'Well, Colin would have been about ten when Harry was born. In fact that's when I lost touch with Joyce. Having children of different ages, it does rather throw a spanner in the works of female friendships!' says Sheena, brightly.

'*Have* you met Harry, Colin?' she adds.

'According to Colin, the advertising agency he works for have been doing One Direction's iTunes campaign. Isn't that right, Colin?' says Kate, acidly.

'No idea where you got that from darlin'' says Colin staring straight ahead of him, innocently, before wandering off towards the group of people talking by the French windows.

'Well, unfortunately Colin won't get a chance to meet Harry tonight, either. I was *so* hoping he could be here. His Uncle Bert and little Cousin Sapphire are here, and so many old family friends, but the boys are recording a new album in some studio in Kent and can't get away. Never mind!' says Sheena brightly, adding, 'I do like your dress, dear, it suits you so well.'

'Thanks.' says Kate, flatly, wondering what she's more upset about, not meeting Harry Styles, or realising what an idiot she's been for trusting Colin again after the way he treated her when they were together.

'Oh, you're disappointed that Harry's not here.' says Sheena, kindly. 'You know, it's gone crazy. Since the boys made it in America. I've had to change our landline number three times. And even though Harry moved out over eighteen months ago, I still get groups of fans loitering outside behind the wall. It's a bit of a pain, but I usually give them some biscuits and send them on their way, poor little things.

'No, it's not that. It's not Harry. It would have been nice to meet him. I'm not a fan, but he's...well, he's so famous.'

'Ah, fame. Fame is a price, not a reward, Kate. The fans don't see the other side of Harry's life. He's lost his freedom. He can't walk down the street without getting mobbed. It's no fun. I mean, don't get me wrong. I'm over the moon that financially he's set up for life, now, and I'm so proud of him, what he's achieved at such a young age, but the music industry, it has jaws of steel, it can eat them up and spit them out in pieces. So, as a mother, obviously, I feel very protective of him and very wary of the whole thing.'

Kate is absently watching the group of women standing by the French windows. They're talking conspiratorially now and laughing, unaware of Colin approaching them.

'So, are you two...?' Sheena asks Kate, trailing off.

'We were. We're just friends now. I've got a boyfriend. Only he works away a lot. He's a *model*.' says Kate, lifting her chin slightly, the corners of her lips turning up with pride.

'Oh! Will I have seen him anywhere?'

'He does a lot of work abroad, Tokyo, Milan, Paris. But in England...well he was featured in the last H&M campaign.'

'Oh! I might have seen him plastered on the wall at Highgate tube station then!' laughs Sheena.

'Yes...like Harry.'

'Well, it's not quite the same...' says Sheena, bristling.

Kate glances over to the group of women, now joined by Colin. He's talking so loudly she can hear him from the other side of the room.

'Yeah babes, Ogilvy and Mather. Art director.' barks Colin at Justine.

'Don't call me babes.'

The room suddenly goes quiet, to which Colin is completely oblivious.

'Figure of speech, darlin'. And a compliment.'

'I don't take it as such. I am not your *babes*. Or your *darling*.'

'I'm just messin' with ya. Lighten up! Can't you take a joke?'

Kate takes a slug of her prosecco and glances nervously at Sheena.

'No, not the same as Harry. Of course. Harry is world famous. My boyfriend...'

'Anyway. It's not all about Harry.' says Sheena in a clipped voice.

Colin's voice booms across the room once again.

'And she was stark naked!' he announces, triumphantly. One or two of the assembled women suddenly look at their drinks, another two glance towards one another then glance away, quickly, to hide their embarrassment. Colin stands in the middle of the group, takes a large swig of his Campari and grins, smugly.

'Not a pretty sight, to be fair.'

Colin smirks and refills his glass from the Campari bottle he seems to have acquired.

'I'm not sure we all know one another well enough to be having this conversation.' announces Justine, her dangly earrings trembling as she shifts her weight from one foot, stands upright and unconsciously clenches her fist around the stem of her wine glass.

'Well, nobody really knows anyone, do they? I mean how well do you know your friends? How well do you know your colleagues? My boss is a right cunt for a start.' Colin laughs loudly, seemingly impervious to the gaggle of frosty looks now pointed in his direction.

'Really. Well my brother-in-law will be interested to know that. He's in the industry too...' says Justine, acidly.

'Oh yeah? Who does he work for?'

'Funnily enough, he works at the same agency as you. Ogilvy and Mather. He's their creative director. In other words, your boss...'

'We call each other cunts all the time. Term of endearment.' grins Colin. 'Great bloke.'

'I think we should go.' says Kate.

'Maybe you're right.' says Sheena, looking worried.

Kate walks over to Colin and says 'I have to go. I feel ill.'

'And what the fuck's wrong with you *now?* You're always fucking *ill.* I was just starting to *enjoy myself!*'

'So were we.' says Justine, glaring icily at Colin.

Kate looks Colin in the eye, turns around and walks towards the door. Sheena catches her arm.

'Darling *do* take him with you, won't you? *Please* don't leave him with me.'

'*You* invited him.' says Kate harshly '*And* you made him think that Harry was going to be here.'

'Er...no I didn't' says Sheena, walking over towards Colin.

'Kate wants to go. You can't let her leave alone. I think you'd better accompany her Colin. OK sweetie?'

Colin necks almost a full glass of Campari and slams his glass down,

'Bye ladies. Been a pleasure.'

'It certainly has.' says Justine, coldly.

'Kate - such a dick.' mutters Colin to himself.

By the time Colin gets to the front door, Kate is nowhere to be seen. He walks outside, down the drive and looks down the road. Kate is about a hundred yards away, hailing a cab. She gets in, her lithe legs slipping into the black cavity of the cab before it speeds away.

'Bitch' he mutters. But no-one is listening.

8

LITTLE WHITE LIES

irst Exposure exhibition, *The National Portrait Gallery, London. 11am, Monday, 25th June, 2012.*

I'd like to come to something like this with Alex, I don't understand why he never seems to want to go anywhere interesting with me anymore, all he seems to care about is work, and yet work's become a taboo subject which he doesn't want to discuss. Fuck it. Ohhh, I love that portrait of Grace Coddington by, who is it? Eric Swayne. Fabulous! So many gorgeous portraits in this exhibition. Oh, the Jimmy Page, wonderful! It's the perfect time to come here, first thing on a Monday morning when it's still quiet, no-one around. Why do people always want to go to openings? Openings aren't about art, they're about who's there and how many freebies there are. Oh, that portrait of Grace Coddington is wonderful, too. Peter Akehurst, 1961. She was so beautiful. She must be in her seventies now...age..

❧❧❧

Fuck fuck fuck, there isn't enough time to squeeze this in, really, with the fitting at Stella McCartney's. I'd like to spend two hours here, not thirty minutes. That's the one, by Neal Preston, 1977. Unbelievable shot. So glad I didn't bother with the opening night, I'd rather see the work on my own whilst it's quiet. But the opening night did give me an excuse not to go to Matt Williamson's do. Matt won't mind, sounds like everyone had a reyt good time.

She reminds me of someone, that woman, but I can't think who. Is she on the tele? Nope, don't think so. She's got that timeless beauty, high cheekbones, elegance...now there's a portrait, Grace Coddington. Gorgeous.

෩෩෩

An ear-piercing alarm shrieks in short, staccato, electronic bleeps. A uniformed guard marches into the room and says abruptly 'This is a security alert. Please will you vacate the building immediately, there is nothing to worry about, please make your way towards the exit doors.'

Julia turns round, looking startled, and puts her fingers in her ears, before immediately removing them to talk.

'What is it? A bomb?' she asks the guard.

'Please make your way towards the exit. Nothing to worry about, just a security alert.'

Julia joins a small group of people now filing through the huge doorway into the gallery reception hall, which is filling up with office workers and gallery visitors from the other halls. The siren is still screeching and bleeping at a deafening, painful volume. Some of the people waiting to get out of the main doors are panicking and pushing the people in front of them. A pregnant woman with a huge mound of tummy protruding in front of her, a pod fit to burst, is trying to avoid being squashed, and a woman next to her is pushing the people around her away, saying 'Let her through! Can't you see she's pregnant?'

It is obvious to Julia how panic can so easily set into a crowd once fear catches light and spreads like wildfire. Along with several other people, she squeezes through the main entrance, watching the pregnant woman in front of her who is now free from the melee and resting her hand on the wall outside. A guard nearby is shouting 'Please will you move away from the front of the building, please clear the front of the building and make your way down the street.'

As Julia turns to look up and down the street, wondering which way to go, a body is thrown into her with such force it almost knocks her over.

She turns round and in front of her is what can only be described as a vision of utter beauty. A tall, lean man with tousled blonde, curly hair, is straightening himself up and looking towards a man in a suit who's marching arrogantly away from them.

'Fookin' hell, mate, there's no need for that!' he says at the retreating back of the man, who doesn't look round, then the blonde man instantly looks at Julia, who is staring at him with a look of fascinated shock on her face. He recognises her. The beauty with the high cheekbones from the exhibition.

'Sorry luv.' he says 'I didn't hurt ya did I?'

'No! I'm fine. It wasn't your fault...' she switches her glance towards the suit now receding into the distance down Charing Cross Road.

'Thinks he's too important to just wait for a few minutes till everyone can get out.' says Matt.

'I know. What are some people like? Wonder what's gone off? Bomb maybe?'

'No idea, luv.' says Matt, glancing towards his iPhone, which is ringing.

'Hi, yup, no, ah alright, yup no problem. See you tomorrow then. Yeah, fine, bye!'

'I suppose,' says Julia, 'We shouldn't really be hanging around outside, in case it *is* a bomb.'

'I know. We could all go sky high luv!'

People are milling around looking confused, talking, some on their phones, some to other strangers. Nothing like a calamity to get Londoners talking to one another. A couple are arguing with one of the guards. The June sunlight dissipates as a large grey cloud passes overhead and suddenly, there's a chill in the air.

A camera crew appear out of nowhere, point a camera at a small group of people and a reporter shoves a microphone into their faces.

'Oh god, the press. That's all I need.' says Julia.

'Yeah, I don't like 'em either.'

'Well, I'm going to head up towards Soho I think, get a coffee at The French House. May as well get something positive out of my morning off. Guess we're not going to be allowed back in any time soon.'

'Aye, I'm gonna walk up that way too.'

They walk side by side, leaving the throng of people behind them, as approaching police sirens wail, getting closer.

'Good timing. Really don't want to be interviewed.' says Matt.

'I'd have thought that security would have rounded everyone up and prevented them from leaving, although I don't know anything about bomb procedure...'

'Me neither. Glad I'm out of it though...press...authorities, not my thing.'

'Nor mine.' says Julia, smiling up at Matt.

He glances down at her face as they're walking, the sun comes out again and lights her up. Her eyes are smiling as well as her lips. She really is beautiful.

'I was meant to be going for a...to see a client...but it's been cancelled...'

'Oh, dear. What kind of client?'

Matt can't tell her he was off to see Stella McCartney. Her expression will transform in an instant and she'll turn to him with the mask of the fan plastered on her face, awe-struck, lips slightly parted, eyes sparkling with hunger, curiosity and delight. Today, he just can't be arsed.

'I'm a...plumber. It was a customer. Put it off till tomorrow.'

'Oh, right.' says Julia, looking confused. 'You don't look like a plumber.'

'Well, I am. Self-taught n'all.'

'And you're not a Londoner, either, are you? Where's that accent from?'

'Hemel Hempstead, luv.'

'Very funny.'

'Nah, I do live there. But I'm from Wakefield. Up North. Where the sun don't shine. The other side of the world.'

'You'd think so, the way some people behave towards Northerners. I like them. I like their frankness, their sense of humour, their dignity. They're straight-up. And much friendlier than us Londoners.'

'You're not wrong there.'

Matt and Julia are walking along Gerard Street and both are wondering exactly what they're doing, walking side by side and chatting with a complete stranger.

'So...what's yer name, then, if you don't mind my asking?'

Julia pauses for a moment. It's not as though she's a household name, but she doesn't want to have to tread the threadbare carpet of questions and statements which is inevitably unfurled before her as soon as anyone finds out she's a writer. 'Are you published? How did you get published? So, how does the publishing industry work? I've always wanted to be a writer. I've got half a novel in a drawer, I'd like you to read it and tell me what you think.' Julia decides, in a split second, she'll be someone else. This is a complete stranger, after all, what harm can it do?

'My name's Gigi.'

'What a fantastic name! Where'd you get that from, then?'

'It was my mum's favourite film. What's your name?'

'Matt. And I love that film too. I saw you inside the exhibition, actually, looking at the Jimmy Page portraits.'

'Weren't they amazing? Wonderful work. And the Grace Coddingtons.'

'Incredible woman. Beautiful inside and out.'

'Oh, is she? I wouldn't know, I don't know much about her apart from the fact she's an editor at Vogue.'

'Well, I don't, either, really. I...I know someone who's worked with her a few times. Really nice woman apparently.'

As they walk further up Dean Street, the blue, white and red flags outside The French House come into view, fluttering in the summer breeze.

'Well, this is me. Thanks for walking with me. It's been nice.' says Julia.

'Yeah. Same here.'

'Well, I guess I'd...well...look, you can join me for a coffee if you want...'

'Yeah alright.' Matt smiles and his whole face lights up. Julia can't remember the last time Alex smiled at her like that, he always seems so engrossed with something else, talking to people from work well into the evening about some project or other, going straight to bed afterwards, complaining about feeling exhausted, being totally uninterested in anything she, Julia, has to say or what she's doing. Somewhere over the last eighteen months, she and Alex have drifted apart, and she doesn't know how or why or what happened. But something went wrong.

As they walk through the front door into the tiny interior, Julia sighs and says 'Hasn't changed in here for years, for as long as I can remember.'

'When did you first come here, then?' asks Matt.

'Oh, the late seventies, when I first moved to London.'

'I've been coming here about five years. I don't come here often though...'

Matt turns and laughs, a cheeky, chuckling laugh. That's another thing. Alex used to laugh. Nowadays he doesn't even smile, never mind laugh.

The bartender wipes his hands on his scrupulously clean white apron and smiles disinterestedly at the couple. 'Yes?'

'Well, I was going to have a coffee, but quite honestly, after all that fuss, I think I'd like a drink.' says Julia.

'Grand idea. Me too. What'll it be? I'll get 'em.'

'Shall we share a bottle of wine?' asks Julia. 'It's after 10am after all.'

Matt laughs, wondering whether or not she's joking, then decides she isn't.

'What do you fancy?'

'House red will be fine, sweetie.'

Was that luvvy talk? Or is she flirting? Or just being friendly? She's confusing him already, and they've only known one another for half an hour.

'A bottle of house red then?' announces the bartender, and swirls round to fetch it.

There's a brief lull in the conversation as they both watch him uncorking the bottle.

'Actually we're from the same place. I live in Hertfordshire, too.' says Julia, leaning on the bar slightly.

'Really? Whereabouts?'

'Tewin'

'Oooh, posh, eh?'

'Quiet. Which is the way I like it. I work from home, so I need the peace and tranquillity.'

'What do you do, then?'

'I'm an artist.' she says, without a beat.

'What kind of artist?'

'Oils on canvas. Still life. Flowers, fruit. Abstract. Not in the Dutch tradition.'

'No blushing peaches and dewdrops dripping off strawberries, then?'

'Well, I couldn't paint like that if I tried. No, it's more expressionistic.'

'Do you exhibit?'

Julia pauses. She suddenly feels uncomfortable, lying. All he has to do is google 'Exhibition. Gigi. Oils on canvas' on his iPhone whilst she's in the toilets and her cover's blown.

'No, I paint for myself. I'm not known. And I keep off the net.' she adds, hurriedly, deeply regretting the ridiculous spur-of-the-moment decision to lie to this stranger whose company she is suddenly enjoying so much.

'I'm not being funny, but plumbers don't normally ask the question 'Do you exhibit?''

'So what's to say yer can't be a plumber and read the Observer colour supplement as well?' asks Matt, his eyes shining with mischief.

'Nothing. I'm being a snob. Sorry.'

The bartender presents them with the wine and two glasses, and Matt pays the bill. The pub is already almost full, but they find a table in the far corner, underneath a Brassai print of the couple, kissing.

'They haven't changed the prints on the walls for forty years. That's one of the reasons I love this place, its timelessness.' says Julia.

She pours them both a glass of wine and smiles.

Her eyes are so full of life and kindness and humour. She must be over fifty, thinks Matt, but her skin is soft and the few wrinkles she has make her face come alive, like a close-up of a leaf where you can see all its intricacies, rather than the flat, shiny green thing of youth.

'How old are you?' asks Julia, as if reading his mind.

'Twenty-five.'

'Oh...just a bit older than my daughter, she's twenty-five'

'How old are *you*, then? You don't look old enough to have a daughter my age!'

Julia laughs shyly, aware that whenever anyone says this, it's more compliment than fact. Matt looks at her eyes and loves the way the lines crinkle around them as she smiles.

'Fifty-six.'

'Never! My mum's younger than you! Only she dun't look it! Sorry, Mum!' says Matt, looking upwards and opening his hands, palms facing upwards at the ceiling.

'So, have you just got the one daughter then? You and your husband?'

'Just my daughter, yes. My husband died a few years ago.'

'Oh, I'm sorry, luv.'

'It's OK.'

'So, does she live at home? Or are you on your own?' Matt laughs. 'I sound like a fookin' stalker now. I've only just met you, sitting in a pub and asking you if you live alone! Er, sorry for swearin''

Julia laughs. 'It's fine. No, she lives with her boyfriend. And I don't live alone. I live with my new partner.'

'Oh, so you found love again, well, that's really nice.' says Matt with a genuine smile.

'I *did* find love. I'm wondering exactly where it went though. Things aren't really working out. My partner is of the disinterested sort, so I've been throwing myself into my work.'

'Painting it out of your system, so to speak!'

'Kind of.'

'Well, I'm in t' same boat if I'm honest. My girlfriend doesn't seem to give a shit. I think all she cares about is being seen wi' me...I mean...'

'It's OK, don't worry about being immodest. I'm old enough to be completely impartial and let's face it, you're a gorgeous looking bloke. Really, you should be a model.'

'Aye, I've heard that life i'nt what it's cracked up to be, though. I was a model once, actually, for some art students, at one of their life drawing classes. Hard to sit still for that amount of time. Wish I'd been able to keep one or two of their drawings, they were great.'

'Where was that, then?'

'St Martins.'

They both take a long draught of their wine, and Matt refills their glasses.

'It seems strange,' says Julia, 'Sitting in a pub, drinking wine with some young bloke. I mean, I've just literally picked you up in the street, kind of! I've gone mad!' and she laughs and her eyes light up again, then she looks away, shyly, and now Matt notices her breasts, round and firm underneath her tight yellow t-shirt, and, against his will, he wants to touch them.

'And he's even younger than Alex! Five years younger! What, am I turning into some ghastly, predatory old woman, pouncing on young men?' thinks Julia to herself before turning back to look at Matt, and catching him as his eyes dart from her breasts over into the middle-distance, as if that's where he was looking all along, although they both know that he wasn't.

'Eh, it wouldn't seem so odd if I were fifty-summat and you were twenty-summat, would it? Happens all the time!'

'I know, but that's about power. Most of those women are only with the older man for two things. His power or his money. I don't think that's why you're sitting here, right now.'

Julia looks Matt straight in the eye with the faintest trace of a smile on her lips, and his heart melts.

'Well, we are where we are.' he says, noncommittally, and smiles at her.

Julia pours the last of the wine into their glasses and sighs.

'It feels like we're on an island, in the middle of nowhere.'

'Isn't that how The French House is meant to make you feel? That's what it is. A little island in the middle of Soho. In the middle of London, in the middle of England, in the middle of the earth, in the middle of nowhere...'

'In the far reaches of the galaxy...' says Julia, quietly, then tilts her glass up and drains it. 'I must go. I *must* go. This wine has gone straight to my head.'

'And mine.' says Matt. 'I'd wine you then I'd dine you, if I could...' he looks at Julia and they both hold their gaze a fraction of a second longer than they would do if they weren't both feeling the same degree of desire for one another.

'Matt, I'm very flattered. And I'd love to go to dinner with you. But I'm living with someone. And you have a girlfriend, too.'

'Living with her...yes...me too...'

'So I think dinner would be out, much as I'd love to.'

Matt looks at her levelly. 'We haven't seen the exhibition yet...'

Julia bites her bottom lip and raises her eyebrows, smiling and then letting out a little laugh. 'That's a point. We haven't...'

9

THE MIRAGE

ven by the evening, it's as though nothing happened that morning.

Julia leaves Matt outside The French House having swapped mobile numbers. They don't kiss one another goodbye on the cheek, but merely reach out a hand towards one another and brush fingertips as they part.

The train journey home is swamped with emotion. What just happened back there? A security alert, bumping into a stranger, going for a drink, and suddenly feeling more intimacy than she's felt since she met Alex, eighteen months ago. But with a boy. A mere child. Only he isn't a child, is he? He's a fully grown man, taller than her, with broad shoulders, a man too old to be the youngest on a battlefield.

'What is it?' Julia asks herself, 'That you're bored with sex with Alex? Bored with conversation? No, it's that the Alex I met has gone. He's somewhere else, I know he is. His mind has left the building. Maybe he's thinking of someone else. Maybe he, too, has fallen in love. He too, Julia? He too?'

Julia knows what she wanted to happen late that morning. There is no hiding place from it. She wanted a hiding place, right in the centre of London, for her and Matt. A deserted, leafy side street.

The sun comes out again as they turn off Dean St down a narrow road, Meard Street, lined with houses, cafes and a single tree. Half way down, just past the Palms of Goa restaurant, is a tiny alley between the houses. Julia and Matt enter the alley. It is paved with cobble stones lit by the sun above, and at the end, opens out into a small private courtyard, framed with cherry blossom trees whose petals have already fallen, covering the ground in a sheet of dappled pink. Spring has come late this year.

Matt takes Julia by the hand and electricity shoots through her body, just the touch of his skin against hers. He pushes her against one of the trees, looks her in the eye with a look almost of sadness, such is the depth of his desire, and kisses her deeply on the mouth. The only sound is birdsong which has silenced the roar of the traffic beyond. Matt presses his body against Julia's, and she can feel his erect penis beneath the cotton fabric of his cargo pants, pressing against the top of her groin through her summer dress. She breaks off the kiss and buries her face in his neck, kissing his skin. He smells faintly of an after-shave she's never smelt before, and she rubs her nose into the curls of his blonde hair. He pulls her head back, gently, and looks at her again, then whispers 'I want you, so much, you're beautiful, Julia.'

'I want you too. Make love to me, right here.'

Matt pulls at the fabric of Julia's dress, lifting it up and sliding one hand underneath and placing it in between Julia's bare legs. She shifts her stance slightly so that her legs are parted and he slides his hand all the way up the inside of her thighs until he reaches her knickers. He slips his fingers underneath the soft silk and places his hand on the fur of her pubic mound, then arches his fingers down and cups her vulva in his hand. It feels hot and is already moist and sticky. Julia gasps with pleasure and longs for him to fuck her. She reaches down and unbuttons his jeans, pulling them down to his thighs. She looks down and there is a sticky dark patch of semen, colouring the front of his underpants. She can't wait, she wants to see his cock, and peels the fabric of his pants down, releasing it. It stands upright, the end engorged and bright red with desire. Julia thinks she's going to faint with pleasure. She glances up at his eyes and he's smiling at her. 'I want you.' he whispers. He's moving his hand on her vulva, squeezing it gently, and Julia is so aroused she feels like she's going to come at any moment.

'Fuck me. Now. I can't wait any longer.' she whispers.

Matt pulls Julia's knickers down to her knees and she wriggles and slips them off. He cups the mounds of her buttocks in his hands and pulls her towards him, raising her up. There is a grey rock at the base of the tree, about a foot high, with a top worn flat from others' bodies, and Julia steps lightly up on it, parting her legs as Matt pulls her towards him and guides his penis towards the opening of her pussy. With one long thrust he pulls her onto him and pushes his cock deep into her. She gasps again and he kisses her deeply on the mouth. She is in heaven. With one hand caressing her bottom, he uses the other to push her shoulder against the tree to steady himself whilst he starts thrusting deep within her. She feels such ecstasy that she can hardly breathe as he pushes his penis into her before withdrawing it and plunging into her once again. She breaks off their kiss and throws her head back, her lips parted, her eyes closed, as he fucks her, his rhythm increasing in speed as he feels his orgasm approaching. She can feel his penis distend in unbearable arousal as he plunges into her again and again and again and waves of pleasure pulse from her vagina up through her belly, infusing her whole body with ecstasy, as he gasps and groans, his eyes widening, looking into hers, his beautiful blue eyes, she's lost, she's swimming, she's sinking, she's flying in his body and eyes and he cries out 'Julia' and pumps into her, long, arching spurts of semen, unseen, pulsing deep into her body. He keeps fucking her until his orgasm subsides and then holds her tightly, kissing her deeply once again on the mouth.

Time passes and Julia opens her eyes. She and Matt are sitting on the rock, fully clothed, her head tilted onto his shoulder, looking up at the sky as clouds scud past a backdrop of vivid blue haze.

Julia turns her head and looks at the voile curtains flapping gently against the French windows. Her pussy is aching with emptiness and she longs to have it filled. She doesn't feel at all satisfied, she feels ravenous, almost delirious with desire for this stranger she has met only once. She only knows one thing at that moment. She has to see him again.

10

JEALOUSY

he flat looks clean, calm and vaguely sterile in the early evening sunlight which slants through the Venetian blinds, casting beams of light onto the surfaces of the open-plan kitchen lounge.

A key turns in the lock and Kate walks in from work, throws her bag down on the kitchen work-surface, kicks off her high-heeled shoes, walks over to the sofa, slumps into it, grabs the remote control and turns the tele on. She doesn't care what's on, anything will do. *Come Dine With Me*, perfect.

One of the contestants in the show leans over a dining table with her cleavage showing, and says 'I got ravaged over the kitchen table this morning!' and the other contestants all splutter into laughter with shock. God, where do they get these people from? Kate checks her iPhone for tonight's show. Sheffield. Typical. Northerners. They're so common.

She can't wait for Matt to come home so she can find out how his fitting went at Stella McCartney's. *Stella McCartney!* Maybe Stella was actually in the studio today!

After the show finishes (the woman with the cleavage wins it, how very predictable) Kate gets up and walks into the bedroom to change out of her work suit. Matt is lying on the bed, on his back, fully clothed, snoring.

'You're home early.' she snaps.

Matt takes a deep breath and slowly opens his eyes, blinking and adjusting them to the light.

'Oh, Kate. Hi.'

'I thought you weren't going to be finished at Stella's till this evening. You said it would take all day.'

'Ah, right. Well...' he says, rubbing his eyes. He looks out of the French window towards the balcony and the trees in the communal garden beyond. The balcony where he'd first kissed Kate, where he'd made love to her. It seems like such a long time ago. He feels exhausted.

'How come you were sleeping during the day? You're not ill, are you?'

'No, luv. Not ill. Just tired.'

'So how did it go at Stella's?' demands Kate, undressing and dropping her clothes onto the bed. Matt rolls off the bed and sits on the side, still looking out of the window, his back to Kate.

'Oh...well, it was cancelled till tomorrow.'

'Oh. I see. What's for tea? I presume you've used your time wisely and made something nice, considering some of us have been working all day.'

'Um...I picked up some wild mushrooms from Covent Garden. Thought we could have them fried in olive oil and garlic. Chicken of the Woods, they're called.'

'Do they taste like chicken?'

'Nah. Not really. They have a lovely firm texture, though.'

'Good. I hope they're not slimy.'

'They're not. Are you hungry, then? Shall I start cooking?' says Matt, getting up and walking past her as she slides her knickers off, dropping them on the floor.

'Please. I'm going to have a shower. It was sweaty today.'

'Yeah...'

Matt runs his fingers through his hair and looks at himself in the mirror. He looks different, but he can't tell why. He feels different.

Kate lays the table whilst he cooks, pouring herself a large glass of chilled white wine.

'D'you want white?' she says across the lounge to the kitchen, where steam is rising from the cooking.

'Put the cooker hood on, Matt. Do you want white?'

'White, yes. Whatever.'

He brings two plates of fresh tagliatelli to the table, topped with orange and yellow garlicky mushrooms which glow with a slick of oil.

'Oh. How odd.' says Kate, flatly, looking at the brightly coloured fungi and taking a large slurp of wine. 'So. No fitting today. Will Stella be there tomorrow?'

'I doubt it. Think she's in Milan till the weekend.'

'I was really hoping you could take a pic, of you and her, put it on Instagram.'

'Kate. You just don't do that, it's really frowned upon. Fittings are Instagram-free zones, this is classified stuff, it's for the new collection.'

'Tiresome.' snaps Kate. 'All so top-secret and hushy-hushy, lovey-lovey, honestly. Anyway, so what did you do today then, if you weren't at the fitting?'

'Well...I went to the National Portrait Gallery, to see that exhibition.'

'The one you were so *desperate* to attend the opening of you mean? The one you used as an *excuse* to miss the Matthew Williamson party? The opening you then *didn't even bother to attend*, whilst Tanya and I had to *fend for ourselves* at the party where *everyone was up their own arses* and *ignored* us? *That exhibition?*'

'Yeah. That one.'

'So was it worth it? All the excuses and fuss and drama?'

'Well, I didn't get to see much of it, actually.'

'Why not?'

'Because there was a security alert. I only got a chance to look at a couple of portraits before the alarm went off and they evacuated the building.'

'Oh!' says Kate, vaguely interested, stuffing a large fork-load of mushrooms into her mouth.

'What's it like?'

'OK. Not really as nice as Marks and Spencer's mushroom pasta. You can't beat Marks and Spencer.'

'It's *fresh*, Kate. You can't beat *fresh*.'

'*Nothing* beats Marks and Spencer. So, what did you do?'

'Well. I was standing outside...' Matt looks out of the window, reliving the moment when he was shoved into Julia by the wanker in the suit, and when she first turned to look at him with that look of shock and curiosity on her face.

'And?...'

'And people were shoving each other, trying to get out of the building.'

'I thought you said you were already out of the building.'

'I was, but people were still coming out and there was a crowd...office workers, tourists, you know...'

Kate stares at Matt as he continues looking out of the window.

'And? So, what happened? You look like you're about to tell me something really interesting. Which so far, it hasn't been.'

'It's not interesting really. Just that some bloke, some office knobhead, bumped into me, and shoved me right into this woman, nearly knocking her over. And we got talking...'

'How old was she?'

'I dunno. Old. Fifties?'

' What did she look like? Was she attractive?'

'No, not really. Plain. I didn't notice, Kate. I was in the middle of a bomb scare.'

'So what were you talking about?'

'The bomb scare. She actually asked me, 'Do you think it's a bomb?''

'She was flirting with you.'

'No she wasn't, it was just an innocent question.'

'No older woman asks a fit bloke like you a question like that without it being *loaded*. Don't be such an *idiot*, Matthew.'

'Kate, it wasn't loaded. We were both a bit shook up from the evacuation, a bloke shoved me into her, which shook her up a bit more, and she wondered what was happening.'

'I bet she did. So, what happened then? She told you she'd got an hour to spare and asked you for a drink...' says Kate, rolling her eyes sarcastically.

'It wasn't *exactly* like that.'

Kate puts her fork down and stares at Matt accusingly.

'What do you mean? You *did* go for a drink with her?'

'We ended up walking the same way, up Charing Cross Road, and we got talking, about the bomb scare, and the exhibition, the little we'd seen of it. And we ended up outside The French House and she wondered if I fancied a coffee...'

'*What?*'

'Sophia had just rung cancelling the Stella fitting and quite honestly I did fancy a coffee. Only once we got in, we had wine instead.'

'You had *wine?* What time was this?'

'About eleven. Look, it was just nice to sit down after all the hassle and crowds outside the gallery and I did have some time to kill before I popped in on Bill at Covent Garden. It was just a drink.'

'How much? I mean, how many drinks? How long were you there?'

'We shared a bottle.'

'A *bottle?* In the *morning?*'

'It *was* after ten o'clock. Look, it just felt like the right thing to do.'

'*After ten o'clock?* What *planet* are you on? Well it was *not* the right thing to do Matthew, it was the *wrong* thing to do.'

'So speaks Miss Half a Bottle of Gin...'

Kate puts her cutlery into her half-finished bowl of pasta and mushrooms, tops up her glass and glares at Matt, silently.

'How attractive was she? Be honest because I know you're lying. You wouldn't go for a coffee with a *munter*.'

'OK she wasn't plain. She was attractive. For her age.'

'So, correct me if I'm wrong here. You went to The French House to share *a bottle of wine* with some *woman* you'd just met who you were *attracted* to. Right?'

'No! Look, you asked me to be honest! I'm sure other men find her attractive but of course I didn't, because I'm with you!' says Matt in an exasperated tone.

Kate narrows her eyes and goes in for the kill.

'What were her breasts like?'

'*What?* I don't fucking know! I didn't even notice them!'

'*That's it.*' she hisses. 'You're a fucking *liar*. No man sits and has a drink with a woman they admit they find attractive without noticing her *breasts. Ever.* It just *doesn't happen.*'

'Look, luv. I spend most of my working days surrounded by some of the most beautiful women in the world who think nothing of wandering round backstage topless. Tits lose their meaning when they're shoved in your face day after day.'

'I don't believe you. You're lying. You fancied her didn't you?'

'No. I did not. And I don't know where you think you get the right to attack me for having a drink with a stranger when last week you went to a party with your ex!'

'That was different and you know it. I only went because it was Harry Styles' party. That is the only reason. You know I can't stand Colin.'

'But you'll use him to get to a party, just like you fucking use me.'

Matt slams his glass down and gets up from the table, whisking the plates away and dumping them in the sink with a loud crash.

'I don't know why you're losing your temper. It's not *me* who's been swanning round Soho with middle-aged frumps gagging over them. It makes me feel faintly nauseous, actually. In fact, you're no better than my mother. The way she's behaved with Alex!'

'Don't be ridiculous. *Nothing happened.*'

Kate stands up and walks towards the kitchen, glass in hand and leans on the kitchen work-surface.

'So what did you talk about then?'

'Nothing much. Her job.'

'Why, what does she do?'

'She's an artist. An oil painter.'

'I see. And what was her name?'

'Gigi.'

'Gigi' says Kate, acidly. 'Gigi.' she repeats, turning it over in her mouth to see what it tastes like. 'Gigi.'

'Yeah...Gigi.' says Matt, and immediately wishes he hadn't said her name, because, against his will, the way he says it sounds gentle.

'So you *do* fancy her.' says Kate. 'Gigi *my arse.* I bet that's not her real name.'

'Why would she lie?'

'I don't know, you tell me, you know so much about this desperate, wrinkled old *cougar.*'

'We just had a drink, Kate. It's not the crime of the century, especially not since you went out with Colin wearing that little white dress. Eh? Sauce for the goose an' all that?'

'I forbid you to ever have any more contact with her. She didn't invite you to be a Facebook friend did she? No, she's probably too old to go on Facebook. She better not have given you her number. You better not have given her *your* number! *Did you?*'

'No, of course not.' lies Matt, tired of the questions and what he sees as a very unfair row. 'I'll never see her again. It was just one of those daft things, a chance meeting, nowt in it so stop worrying about it.'

'Did you tell her about me?'

'Yes. And she's living with her partner. She wasn't on the pull, Kate.'

'Right.'

'She was just being friendly.'

Kate feels the bile rising in her stomach. So he didn't notice her breasts, and she was 'Just being friendly'. What more proof does she need that this woman, whoever she is, is a threat?

11

GIGI

he French windows are ajar and the transparent, white, voile curtains waft back and forth gently in the breeze. Matt gently surfaces to consciousness from a deep sleep and notices the branches of the trees in the garden beyond the curtains, swaying and rustling from the movement of air. A face is before him, hovering in his mind, smiling, the upturned lips gentle and soft, the eyes warm and lucid. It's that woman, Gigi. He realises that he's woken up thinking of her, before noticing an absence of Kate next to him in the bed, and feels nothing but relief. As he awakens fully, looking out of the window at the blue sky daubed with clouds moving slowly across its surface, he suddenly realises that it's over with Kate.

He doesn't quite know what's brought about the realisation, but now he can see her as she is, a selfish user who doesn't belong in his life. Somehow, meeting the stranger Gigi has crystallised everything about Kate, transformed her from a quirky tangled ball of enchanting mystery into a spoilt selfish brat. How could he have been so stupid? How come he didn't see it coming? How did he ever fall for her? And what is she doing living in his flat?

He doesn't even want to waste his time thinking about her. She's now just a mechanical problem, to be addressed and sorted out. Thank fuck he hasn't had to see her this morning and she's already gone to work. Right now, with an hour to spare before he has to get up to go to London, all he wants to do is think about this mysterious woman, Gigi.

Her face floats before him again, her smile and the warmth in her eyes. He can feel his cock hardening once again after his thinking about Kate had caused his usual early morning erection to instantly subside.

He pushes the sheet back and watches it grow until it stands upright from his body, long and thick and firm, the glans protruding, hot scarlet and shiny from the drawn-back foreskin. Without thinking he wraps his right hand around the shaft and starts gently pumping it back and forth, closing his eyes to let Gigi's face and breasts swamp his mind with longing and lust.

⅔⅔⅔

Lying there naked before her, his arm propped up on a pillow, his legs stretched out on the chaise longue, he's concentrating on not getting a hard-on as she scrutinises his body. She's sitting on a stool, facing an easel on which is a canvas, ready to paint him. She's wearing a man's shirt, perfectly white and pristine, unbuttoned to the waist, so that he can see the bulge and curve of her breasts beneath the fabric. Her nipples are stiff and protrude through the thin cotton. She starts painting, glancing over at him every now and then, dipping her brush into the silky coloured oils on her palette and then dashing the canvas with colour. She tilts her head to one side and thoughtfully flicks her bottom lip back and forth with her finger as she looks between him and the canvas. Her lips are swollen and plump, as though she's already aroused.

She stands up, and, dreamlike, glides over towards him.

'Your leg isn't quite right' she says, reaching over and slipping her hand in between his thighs, parting them, then moving his legs slightly apart. As she bends down, the fabric of her shirt slips open further, and he can see the outline of her entire breast, heavy and large, resting gently in its cotton sheath with the pink nipple, stiff and enticing, pushing against the cotton and making a little peak in its surface. He is desperate to reach into her shirt, peel it from her shoulders and take her full, warm breasts in his hands, cupping them and running his hands over them.

She stands up, walks back to her easel and sits on the stool, parting her legs. She is wearing only the shirt, now completely open, revealing both large, heavy breasts, sculpted in exquisite, sensuous beauty, just waiting for him to touch them. She isn't wearing knickers and her parted legs reveal a triangle of hair with the folds of her vulva just visible at its base, glistening with her arousal.

She looks him in the eye then looks down at his body and notices his erection, now.

He can't help it, he has to touch his aching cock. He runs his fingers up and down the length of the shaft before grasping it tightly. Her eyes gaze at him meltingly as she slips her hand between her parted legs, moving her fingers down to her vulva, and starts massaging the glistening folds of flesh with the tip of her middle finger.

'I want to see you come.' she murmurs, her voice deep, almost hoarse.

He starts pumping his cock back and forth with regular movements and immediately feels overwhelmed by the pulses of desire shooting through his body. She smiles as she arches her back and her breasts jiggle slightly with the movement. She stretches her legs even wider as she continues to gently caress her vulva with one hand, then with the other, cups both of her breasts in her arm and runs the fingers over her stiff nipples.

He is pumping his cock fast now with a regular rhythm, back and forth, as his breathing becomes heavier and his eyes start to glaze over.

'Don't come.' she orders. She pulls her hand from between her legs and stands up, shrugging the shirt from her shoulders, revealing her body in its mature, fully blossomed beauty, her breasts still round and firm, her hips broad, her tummy soft, her whole body electrifyingly inviting. She walks over to him, lifts one leg up and over his thighs and kneels astride him, looking him in the eye and smiling slightly.

She moves her hand down between his thighs and starts stroking them, running her fingers up and down his flesh, causing waves of desire to shoot through his entire body.

Her heavy breasts are inches from his face. He moves his hands up towards them and cups them in both hands, then rubs the palms of his hands over their soft surface, pausing to lightly move his fingers over her erect, pink nipples.

He has never longed for a woman like this before. She's a goddess, almost other-worldly. He can smell the fragrant musk of her pussy and he is desperate to fuck her.

As if sensing the depth of his desire, she slides her hand slowly up his thigh to his straining cock, wraps her fingers around it tightly and guides it into her pussy, pushing down on him as he sinks back with sheer relief as the warm, moist folds of her flesh encase his throbbing penis. She cups his face in her hands, then kisses him deeply on the mouth, her lips soft and parting, her tongue deliciously moist and erotic, before pulling away from him again. She places her hands on his shoulders and holds him down then thrusts her hips towards him, encasing the entire length of his cock inside her before pulling away again and teasing him by moving her oily pussy across the tip of his cock before plunging it back into her again with another thrust of her hips.

She starts riding him with a regular, urgent rhythm now and her breasts, still cupped in his palms, bounce gently up and down with the movement.

Gigi

He feels as though he's going to explode, she's inside him, all over him, on top of him, under his skin, he's been engulfed in the swirling aura of Gigi. Every time she lowers herself onto him, he can feel his cock pushing to the very depths of her vagina, which encases him tightly with oily fluidity. He is so overcome with pleasure his other senses have all but vanished, he can now neither hear nor smell anything, his whole mind and body is rushing towards a vortex of pure lust for Gigi, her velvet body and her gently bouncing breasts.

As she holds him down by his shoulders he can feel his orgasm shoot through his body as he pumps out long spurts of come deep inside her. She gasps and lets out a long sigh as her own floods of warm liquid flow around his cock, then she falls down onto him, her breasts now pressed against his chest, and runs her fingers through his hair.

She whispers his name, softly, 'Matt.'

ᘓᘓᘓ

'*Matt.*' The harsh tone of Kate's voice penetrates the air like a thunderclap. He is lying on his back, his hand resting on his stomach which is covered with a slick of now transparent spunk.

'I see. You haven't wanted to fuck me for weeks so you're *having a wank.* Brilliant.'

'No I wasn't. I thought you were at work.'

'Yes, you *were.* You're *disgusting.* Good job I had to come back for some brochures I'd forgotten, isn't it, otherwise I'd never have *known!*'

'For fuck's *sake* Kate, we've both been busy, we've hardly seen each other.'

'Because you've been too busy taking old crones for drinks, that's why!'

'That was one morning. Look, I don't want a row. So I felt a need to clear the custard. Big deal.'

'*Clear the custard*? You're disgusting, you know that? When I met you I thought you were really classy. Elegant, you know. But you're just a *pig.*'

'So you never masturbate then? Eh, Kate? Never flick the bean? Never paddle the skin boat? Hmmm?'

'I'm never in the fucking *mood*, because I'm so *neglected*. How you could let me and Tanya go to Matthew Williamson's party...'

'Oh, we're onto *that* again are we? For fuck's sake Kate, why don't you just fuck off to work and give me a fucking break.'

'I think I will. And this room stinks. Of *men*.' she yells, with finality.

Kate storms out of the room and slams the front door on her way out. How come he never heard her key in the door or the front door open? He was lost. Lost in Gigi, in her breasts, her body.

'I have to see her.' he thinks.

He reaches over and grabs his iPhone and starts composing a text.

gigi hi, do you fancy catching that exhibition again? i'm going to try again next monday, same time, 10am, when it's quiet.

He punches send. Seconds later his phone vibrates. A text and the name Gigi.

sure. see you there. great x

Fuck. This is it. He's going to see her again. Fuck fuck fuck fuck fuck *fuck*!

12

INCOGNITO

 *igi, hi, are you still ok for today? 10am in the exhibition room? there's a great review of it in the guardian – from coddington to page it's called, no way, they were the ones we liked! x*

No, I don't feel fucking guilty. I'm going to see an exhibition with someone. Kate won't be around anyway, she's working late tonight, and she's been going to parties with her ex. Who has probably still got a thing about her. And is a complete wanker. I mean, it's humiliating, apart from anything else. I don't know what's got into her. I do everything I can to please her, work hard, pay most of the bills, cook for her, stack the dishwasher, mop the floor. Obviously she thinks I'm eye-candy when we go out, there's that, yeah, a trophy boyfriend, that's probably all I am to her.

Fuck, I don't want to admit it to myself most of the time but I've been struck with the curse of every model I've ever met. Being a trophy girlfriend or boyfriend to someone who reels you in with the bait of 'Yes, you're gorgeous, but I'm not interested in your looks. It's you that fascinates me, the you inside, the real you.'

And then you find out after weeks or months that they're just like all the rest. All they care about is using you to make them feel better about themselves, to lap up the shocked, adoring looks wherever you go as a couple. 'Wow, he must have something about him to be with her!' and 'What has she got that I haven't that she gets a supersonic stud-muffin like him?'

It's vaguely depressing. In fact, it's very depressing.

This woman, this Gigi, talked to me as an equal, and wasn't banging on about my looks. She was real.

❧ ❧ ❧

gigi, hi, are you still ok for today? 10am in the exhibition room? there's a great review of it in the guardian – from coddington to page it's called, no way, they were the ones we liked! x

Oh god, it's here, today! What am I going to wear? That sixties vintage dress with the bluebells on, that'll be fitting. This is really idiotic. He is twenty-five! A baby!

Julia looks at herself in the mirror. The face that for so many years looked back at her was unlined with peachy skin. Now it's lined and dotted with blemishes, from the sun, from an unhealthy lifestyle, liver spots, she's got no idea, but it looks old. A little girl in the street referred to her as an 'old lady' the other day.

An old lady is looking back at her now through the mirror, quietly asking her what the hell she's up to, whilst she unconsciously plans to throw herself at a man young enough to be her son. Even younger than Alex. It's not right. But it feels right. It feels exciting, and fun, and spontaneous. Plus, he is gorgeous.

❧ ❧ ❧

gigi, hi, are you still ok for today? 10am in the exhibition room? there's a great review of it in the guardian – from coddington to page it's called, no way, they were the ones we liked! x

That *fucking bastard*! 'Never going to see her again?' Yeah, fucking right! So he's arranged to meet up with this 'Gigi' to go back to that fucking exhibition. *Twat*. Well he's not getting away with it. *Bastard*.

꿏꿏꿏

Kate puts Matt's iPhone back on the bed before he gets out of the shower. What an absolute *cunt*. She decides there and then what she's going to do. She's going to go to the gallery in disguise and spy on them. Childish, maybe. Creepy and stalkerish, definitely, but she doesn't care.

Matt emerges from the bathroom into the bedroom ruffling his wet, curly hair with a towel and walks past Kate who's sitting on the bed, flicking through a copy of July's *Tatler*. His naked torso looks fantastic, toned, slightly tanned, firm and with glowing, healthy skin. She hates him.

'I won't be getting home till late tonight, remember?' says Kate, casually. 'What are you doing?'

'Dunno. I'll be in London. Depends what comes up.'

I bet it does.

Well, I'll cook when I get in.' answers Kate.

'Mmm. Whatever, yeah.'

Tosser.

Unusually, Matt shuts the front door softly when he leaves for work. Usually he slams it. Kate picks up her mobile and rings work. She's loath to pull a sickie, especially with so many properties on completion day today, but this is serious. Her relationship is stake. Which means her entire life is at stake.

Kate picks up her iPhone and rings Geoff, her boss. It goes to voicemail.

'Geoff darling, I can't make it in today. I've picked up that *awful* virus that's going round and I feel *terrible*. I'm staying in bed but ring if you need to. Leave a message if you don't get through, I might be asleep.'

She knows she can't turn up at the gallery wearing her usual clothes and hair. She's going to have to go in disguise. This is going to take some preparation.

'I'll go to Bloomsbury's and get myself a wig. And Camden Market round the corner and get some boho shabby-chic stuff. ' she thinks. Suddenly, she feels in control. She's made a decision. She's not going to just stand by and let Matt take the piss out of her like this. She's going to actually *do something about it.*

჻ ჻ ჻

London is already stiflingly hot, embracing its warmth and keeping it cloaked and huddled in its narrow streets, stretched and baked on its long avenues. When Julia emerges from Charing Cross tube, she's already perspiring slightly and feels the grime and heat of London's streets wash over her in an unpleasant wave.

Walking into the air-conditioned reception hall of The National Portrait Gallery, she suddenly feels safe and cocooned in its history and coolness. She's five minutes early. Her heart is beating fast. She wants to see Matt, no, not just wants, she's *longing* to see him. This complete stranger.

She waits for him in the hall, standing in a vacuum of space and time, the world suspended in time.

He walks through the door, grinning at her and her heart lurches. As he walks towards her, she suddenly realises without any doubt that this is a date.

He looks unbelievably beautiful. He's wearing a tight white Kid Acne t-shirt, jeans and black, ankle-length leather boots. The t-shirt has 'South Yorks' written on it in scrawled italic lettering above a black and white comic book image of a couple, kissing. Julia feels frumpy by comparison in her vintage summer dress and low-heeled shoes.

'Hi, Gigi,' he smiles, and wraps his arms around her, hugging her, before kissing her lightly on the cheek.

'Hello Matt.' says Julia, and sighs, unable to repress a huge, open-mouthed grin.

'You look stunning. Love the frock. It's vintage, isn't it?'

'Yeah. Sixties. Like my mother used to wear.' she laughs, lightly. 'Shall we go in?'

'That's what we're 'ere for.' answers Matt in his broad, Yorkshire dialect.

Julia feels peace, she feels coolness, she feels full, she feels empty, she feels desire, confusion, lust and excitement all at once, and it feels good.

They walk in, side by side, like a couple.

The exhibition room is empty but for a handful of Japanese tourists in a tight clutch down the far end of the room, earnestly moving from photograph to photograph and nodding at one another, quietly.

Matt and Julia drift towards the row of photographs lining the wall, some huge enlargements, some small curios, of people famous in their time and famous now but maybe not famous in another fifty years. It occurs to Julia how fleeting life is, that she and this virtual stranger, Matt, are just snatching moments together in a bubble of time which will all too soon be forgotten.

They stand in front of a print of the sixties model Chrissie Shrimpton.

'Gorgeous.' coos Julia.

'Ah bet you looked like that in t' sixties.'

Julia laughs and glances sideways at Matt. 'I was a child then. Chrissie Shrimpton must be seventy now...'

'Wish ah'd been around then, in t' sixties. I bet it were a reyt laugh.'

'For a few fleeting years, yes, and for some...I guess it was a time of change...'

'Aye. Like punk. Ah missed that 'un, too.'

'Yes, but you've grown up with computers...mobile phones. We didn't even have colour tele when I was young.' Julia pauses and laughs again. 'Oh god. 'When I was young.' Listen to me. I have this conversation all too frequently, unfortunately...' she says, walking on to the next section of prints.

'With yer daughter?'

'No...not really...I mean...oh well, just generally...' and Julia feels the weight of regret that she ever lied to Matt in the first place about her circumstances.

She stands in front of a photograph of another iconic sixties model, Pattie Boyd, pushes her bottom lip under her teeth and tilts her head to one side, thinking.

She looks so beautiful and vulnerable, despite her age. She's graceful, intelligent, thoughtful. Unlike Kate. How did he end up with *Kate?* He glances quickly back to the photograph on the wall, so that Julia doesn't think he's staring, which he knows he is.

'I bet she's an interesting person, Pattie Boyd.' Julia leans forwards and reads the information next to the photograph. 'It says here that *Something* and *Layla* are both written about her.'

'Ah didn't know that. She's a reyt nice lass though.'

'How do you know? You've *met* her?'

'Aye. Er...well. Once. Briefly, like...' he tails off, embarrassed.

'How come?'

Matt realises he shouldn't have said anything and inwardly kicks himself for being unable to resist showing off. It's hardly likely he's met Pattie Boyd through being a *plumber.*

'Just...through some people ah know that's all. At some social thing. She just happened to be there.'

Matt also inwardly kicks himself for lying in the first place. This is what grasping, needy, shallow Kate has done to him, made him wary of admitting to anyone what he does for a living. It's bloody ridiculous.

'Is she still beautiful?' asks Julia.

'Oh yes. Age cannot wither her. Like you.' Matt turns to look at her, grinning cheekily.

Julia feels a hot flush rising in her face and reaches up to touch her cheek.

'You've made me blush, Matt. I haven't blushed in...so long...' and she smiles back at him, her eyes sparkling, then laughs and shakes her head, grinning, her blonde hair swinging gently.

Neither of them notice the petite young girl sidle into the gallery. With long, wavy blonde hair and a blunt cut fringe, pale lipstick and huge dark sunglasses, she's wearing a long, brightly coloured tie-dye skirt, cork wedge sandals which make her appear much taller than she is, and a thin, floaty chiffon blouse tied at the waist. She walks casually in the direction of Julia and Matt and stops a few feet to the side of them where she peers at the photographs on the wall whilst glancing slyly to her left at the couple.

'That is fucking *them!* My mother and *Matt!*' a voice is screaming inside her. She can feel her heart pounding and realises that she is inadvertently clenching and unclenching her fists. She forces herself to look relaxed, but Matt and Julia haven't even registered her presence.

'I love it when you laugh. You really are gorgeous, you know.' says Matt in a low voice, glancing around him. The student in his periphery vision, looking at the photographs, is a meaningless blur.

Julia stops laughing, her blush receding now, turns and looks at Matt, who holds her gaze and doesn't look away. He is so incredibly gorgeous, his beautiful clear skin, his piercing blue eyes and the fronds of blonde curls trailing across his face. And those lips. Her eyes move down to his lips which are slightly parted as he looks at her, then glance back up at his eyes. He reaches out both hands and cups Julia's face in his hands, pulling her gently towards him, wrapping his arms around her, then kisses her on the mouth.

Julia falls into his body, completely oblivious to her surroundings, wraps her arms around his waist, pulls him even closer and parts her lips to kiss him back.

As he holds her and she swims into the warm gentleness of his kiss, the room around her recedes into nothingness and her head spins. She hasn't felt this depth of longing, desire and sheer happiness for so long.

❦❦❦

The Japanese tourists at the far end of the room are whispering and glancing at Alex and Julia in a deeply embarrassed fashion. Kate is rooted to the spot, paralysed with disgust.

'I cannot *believe* what I am fucking *seeing*.' she thinks. She wants to march over and grab the pair of them and wrench them apart, but she feels physically sick and starts to feel dizzy. Worried that she might actually throw up in the middle of the gallery, she turns and runs outside. The rush-hour pedestrians hurry past her in the warm evening light and fury mounts inside her as, now that she is no longer confronted by the sight of her mother and her boyfriend in a passionate embrace, the nausea recedes. The tableau before her in the gallery, a grotesque echo of when her mother fell in love with her husband Alex, has filled her with anger and revulsion.

❦❦❦

'Gigi' whispers Matt, and smiles, gently as he breaks away from their long, soft kiss.

Julia pushes her hair back from her face and smiles back, before glancing at the rest of the room, where the Japanese tourists look away quickly. 'What must everyone think of us?'

'They probably think we're madly in love.' laughs Matt.

'Or just mad...' says Julia, raising her eyebrows and grinning.

'Or both...' says Matt, nudging her and laughing again.

'Well, that was lovely. I...'

'Shhh. Don't say a word. No-one saw a thing.'

13

SCORN

hat fucking *cunt!* That fucking *bitch!* Who do they think they *are?* Isn't stealing my husband *enough?* Now my fuck-up of a mother has to steal my *boyfriend? Bitch!* How desperate must she be, to stoop to shagging *a twenty-five year old!* Why doesn't she just behave like other, normal mothers and shag horrible bald old men with paunches? It's what she deserves! She doesn't deserve to have someone fit like Matt! How does she do it, anyway? She's *old!* She's *wrinkled!* She's *flabby!* People who look like that don't even *understand* sex, they know *nothing* about it! Anyway how can *old* people understand *sex?*

The thought of Matt and her mother having sex makes Kate physically want to retch. As if Alex wasn't bad enough.

Kate marches up Charing Cross Road, looking for a cab and hails one almost immediately.

'Bates and Bartle. Soho Square.' she barks.

'Right you are darlin''

The cab swings back into the traffic and Kate's stomach lurches. She stares at the people walking along the street, feeling an angry heat rising in her face. '*Cunt. Bitch.*'

Kate gets out of the cab and hands him fifteen quid. 'Keep the change.' she snaps, archly, hauling herself out of the cab in the swirly skirt, which tangles annoyingly around her legs.

Kate pushes open the double glass doors which have B&B etched into them in gold lettering. The doors open straight into the open-plan office which is mainly deserted apart from one or two people sat back on their chairs in front of shining computer screens.

There is a large desk facing the entrance doors, behind which sits a girl about her age with bright red hair scraped up into a tall bun on the top of her head, and wearing a neat sage green skirt suit. She's wearing a name badge which says 'Jenny Groves. Senior Team Admin.' She hovers her fingers over the Mac Air Book in front of her and looks up at Kate.

'Do you have an appointment?'

A door about thirty feet away opens and Alex walks into the office, closely followed by a tall, lithe, blonde woman wearing a short skirt, high heels and a frilly, chiffon blouse. *Slut.*

Alex stops, turns round and smiles at the woman. She leans towards him, whispers in his ear and he laughs then slides his hand around her waist, dropping it down to her bottom which he squeezes lovingly whilst whispering into her ear. She recoils and bursts into laughter, her face lighting up with delight.

'So...do you have an appointment?' repeats the redhead, less politely now.

'Him...I want to see *him*...Alex Harcourt...' says Kate, seething, barely able to repress her anguish any longer.

'What's your name, please? I'll let him know you're here.' says Jenny with ice-cool composure and a cold smile.

'*He knows who I am!* I need to see him! *Now!*' orders Kate.

Jenny puts a pair of headphones on, punches a button on the screen and connects to Alex on Facetime. 'There's a woman here to see you. She switches the camera view to display Kate, boiling on the spot in her flounces, floppy hat, shades and tight-lipped fury.

'I'm just next to Jack's desk. I can see her from here. Who is she?'

'What's your name?' Jenny repeats.

Scorn

'Kate. His *ex-wife*. Just tell him to get over here! I've got something very important to tell him!'

'Jen, she ain't my ex-wife. I don't know who the fuck she is but tell her I'm busy.'

'He's in a meeting, sorry.' says Jenny, flatly.

'But I can *see* him! He's over *there! Alex!*' shouts Kate.

Sandi strides purposely across the room towards the reception desk and stops in front of Kate.

'I don't know who you are, but Alex is about to go into a meeting and can't see you. If you leave your name he'll get back to you when he's free.'

Kate removes her sunglasses, takes off her hat and rips off her long, blonde curly wig.

'*I'm his ex-wife! I am important and I demand to see Alex right now!*' screeches Kate, finally losing her temper.

Alex marches over to the reception desk, glances at Sandi and says 'It's fine. I'll deal with it.'

'Deal with it? *Deal* with it?' shrieks Kate. 'Oh, so now I'm an *it*, am I? Just a *thing!* Just a transient *object* in your *desperately* busy life which seems to mainly revolve around flirting with *sluts* in your *office!*'

Alex grabs Kate's arm and marches her away from the reception area, out through the double glass doors and down the two steps to the pavement in Soho Square.

'What the *fucking hell* are you playing at Kate? Why are you wearing that *insane* costume? What's got into you?'

'I'll tell you what's got into me, *my fucking mother* who happens to be *your fucking lover,* that's what! Do you know where she is, right now? She's in the fucking National Portrait Gallery sucking face with *my boyfriend*, that's what she's doing!'

'Are you on drugs Kate? What the fuck are you talking about?'

'I've just told you.' says Kate, pushing her face into Alex's. 'My mother has fucking *lost the plot!* And my boyfriend is a *total cunt!* Even more of a cunt than *you*, and that's saying something!'

'Kate, you're hysterical. I don't know what substances you've taken, I don't know what you're talking about, but it's crazy gibberish. You need to go home, have a bath and go to bed.'

'I am not hysterical! I am telling you the truth! I thought you'd want to know! How dare you accuse me of being hysterical!'

'Kate, are you, by any chance, on the blob?'

'No I am not *on the blob!'* Kate screams, as passers by glance at her then quickly look away. 'That is so typical of you! I'm trying to help you! I'm trying to warn you what she's like! That *woman!* My *mother!* How *out of control* she is! What a *liability* she is! And you think I'm *crazy* or having my *period!* You are a fucking *waste* of space, you know that?'

'Go home, Kate, just go home. Seriously.'

Sandi is standing behind the glass doors, glaring out at the street.

'And as for that *slut*. How *dare* you treat my mother like that. You're meant to be her *boyfriend* and you're just tossing it off at your supposed *office* pawing *that* piece of trash. You're *pathetic!'*

Kate turns and stomps a few paces down the street before hailing an oncoming taxi.

'Charing Cross station.' she spits out at the cabbie and climbs in, leaving Alex shaking his head on the pavement, and Sandi strutting down the steps of Bates and Bartle to rescue him from his completely insane ex-wife.

❧❧❧

Kate stands outside the toilet on the train from London to Hemel Hempstead and punches Tanya's number into her iPhone.

'Tanya?'

'Babes! Not heard from you for a while!'

'Oh Tanya it's been awful you'll never believe it...'

'What, babes?'

'Matt. I've just caught him and my mother in the National fucking Portrait Gallery.'

'Doing what? Looking at pictures?'

'No, snogging!'

'No...'

'Yes!'

'Did they see you?'

'No, I was wearing a...kind of disguise. Hippy clothes, so they wouldn't see me. Then I went to Alex's stupid web design place and told him about it and get this! He didn't fucking believe me! He just thought I was having my period!'

'Wanker.'

'I know! I'm doing him a favour, right, telling him? I didn't have to go out of my way and tell him, did I?'

'No babes, you didn't, that was a very selfless thing to do. Charity in fact.'

'I know! That's what I thought!'

'So, are you going to confront your mother? About her and Matt?'

'No, right, I'm not, babes. Not yet. I am fucking furious but if I can spy on them once I can spy on them again. I'm going to find out exactly how far it's gone first...'

'You do right, Kate.'

'Exactly. But after the disgusting way Alex has just treated me, totally humiliating me in front of that snotty up-her-own-arse receptionist and some little slut he was dribbling over, I'm going to frigging well *snitch* on him to *my mum*.'

'Yeah, absolutely babes, absolutely. Let her know what the wanker's up to.'

'I'm going to, don't worry!'

'Who's this slut at work then?'

'Dunno. Blonde. Too thin. Slutty clothes...'

'Like what?'

'Short skirt, heels. Without a platform. About five years out of date. See-through blouse that looked like she got it from Oxfam or something. Extensions. No way that was her real hair.'

'She sounds *common*...'

'She is. Her and Alex were whispering in each other's ears when I arrived. Scumbag.'

'*Bitch.*'

'I know, babes. I feel drained by it all to be honest. I'm going home to have a Bacardi and coke and a hot bath.'

'I'm not surprised, after what you've been through. Babes, wish I was there to give you a hug.'

'Me too.'

'Listen I've got to go. Bell me soon, babes.'

'Will do Tanya. Love ya.'

'Love ya babes.'

14

LUNCH AT STEF'S

eaving one another at the gallery after that first kiss had been difficult. Matt to return home to Kate, sprawled across the sofa snoring loudly with an empty half bottle of gin on the table, a half-full bottle of tonic and a squashed lemon lying on her bare midriff, Julia to go back to an empty house as Alex was working late, not to return until after 10pm, by which time Julia had fallen into a deep slumber after masturbating in bed, imagining Matt there in bed with her, making love to her.

Both had agreed not to see one another for a few days, to let things settle, to see how they felt about one another, to try and put into perspective what was happening to them, but two days later, Julia receives a text.

gigi, can you meet me for lunch tomorrow? i really want to see you. matt x

yes, where do you fancy going? gigi xxx

stefs is nice, off oxford street, italian.

1pm? x

see you there, can't wait x

nor can i xxx

❧❧❧

Unsure of what to wear. Unsure of everything. Her life, her relationship with Alex, which obviously isn't working, her feelings, the fact that Matt is even younger than Alex.

'*Twenty-five!* That is a *child!* He's still so *young*, so *innocent!* He doesn't need seducing, he needs nurturing and protecting... protecting from women like me!' she says to herself in the mirror. She decides on leggings, ankle boots and an almost transparent, floral shirt, which she leaves unbuttoned to reveal her cleavage.

'I shouldn't be doing this. Yes I should. He's an adult. No he's not, he's a *boy!*' her mind races from one thought to the next in confusion. By the time she's on the train to London, her heart is pounding and she feels faint. 'I really should not be doing this. But I *have* to. I *have* to see him.'

※ ※ ※

Matt wakes up feeling unbearably horny and masturbates furiously as soon as Kate has gone to work.

'I want to fuck her. I've got to fuck her. I'm going to fuck her.' He gets up, pulls on a pair of jeans and a faded blue t-shirt and decides to wear his yellow Converse sneakers. Can't go wrong in those. All the way into London he's trying to suppress an uncomfortable erection and has to go to the toilets to rearrange himself.

'How fucking gorgeous is she anyway? Unbelievable. Her breasts. Oh god, try not to look at 'em when you see her Matt, you knobhead.'

※ ※ ※

Matt stands outside the restaurant to wait for her. He wants them to choose a table together. People stride purposefully past and none of them is her, but suddenly he sees her, turning the corner and walking towards him from the direction of Oxford Street. Matt can't help but grin as he watches Julia approach. Her tits look fucking amazing, bouncing gently as she walks, and her face radiates joy and happiness as she sees him. He's stretching out his arms to hold her even before she's reached him, and then throws his arms around her and pulls her close to him. He moves his face near her neck and kisses her lightly on the cheek.

'You smell of coconut.' he murmurs.

Julia looks slightly bashful as she pulls away. 'Oh, yes. Coconut...it's coconut oil...' her voice trails off.

'I thought I'd wait for you out here.'

'No, that's lovely.'

They walk into Stef's' light, clean airy interior and a waiter salutes them from the middle of the room.

'*Bella!*' he shouts in Julia's direction as he walks towards the couple.

'You don'a mind if I call you *Bella?*' he says to Julia in a heavy Italian accent. 'Because you are!' he exclaims, throwing his arms apart and grinning. 'Matt-ah! You return again! You love us here, no?'

Matt grins. 'Best Italian in London.'

'So, you're a regular.' says Julia as the waiter leads them to a table at the back of the restaurant.

'I come here with mates sometimes. Me girlfriend dun't like Italian.' says Matt, matter of factly, as they sit down at a small, square table covered with a pristine white tablecloth and shining silver cutlery.

'No, neither does my daughter.' says Julia, casually, but feels as though his sentence has punched her in the chest. Matt has a girlfriend. She, Julia, has a boyfriend. What are they doing? This is crazy.

But as they sit down and look at one another and smile, the rest of the world dissolves and melts away, leaving just the two of them, stranded on their little island of loving looks, smiles and anticipation.

The waiter brings two menus over to the table and with a flourish presents one to Julia and one to Matt.

'Would you like-a to order drinks now? Or you wait?' he asks, smiling.

'A jug of water. And two glasses.' says Julia. 'Are we having wine as well, Matt?'

'Yeah, white or red?'

'White would be nice with pasta...'

'A bottle of Fiano Solento please, Giano.' says Matt, grinning at the waiter without even looking at the menu.

'I fetch. Lovely to see you here again Signor Matt, with such a *bella donna*.' Giano smiles at Julia and whisks himself away to fetch the wine, cutting out the usual banter with Matt, sensing instinctively that the couple want to be alone.

Matt looks at Julia and grins. She looks back at him and grins as well.

'This is the best thing I've done in ages.' he says.

'I know. It was the right thing to do...'

'We don't know each other do we? We know nowt about each other really. But I feel like I've known you all me life.'

'So do I.' says Julia quietly, looking into his eyes. 'The first time you spoke to me, it felt as though I'd known you from somewhere else...from another life or something...it didn't feel like bumping into a complete stranger. It felt like finally I'd found you, and all this time, I didn't even know I'd been looking for you.'

'Maybe we were together in a past life, if you believe in all that...which I don't really, but you never know. I felt the same though...'

'It felt like we were already bonded somehow, like our lives were already intertwined. When you looked at me...when we walked up Charing Cross Road together, we were strangers... what were we doing walking up the road together? You just don't do that! Especially in London, where everyone's so unfriendly...' says Julia.

'I know, it's not summat I'm in the habit of doing either. It just happened, didn't it? It were like we recognised each other.'

'Has that ever happened to you before?'

'Nope.'

'Not even with your girlfriend?' asks Julia, knowing that she shouldn't really be bringing her up.

'Nah. No...she's...she's a lovely lass...we've never been in love though...I never had that feeling, like I'm having now, of feeling like I've known someone all me life.'

'I'm trying to think back. I don't think I have, either. No, no I haven't. It's the weirdest thing. It's completely taken me aback if I'm honest.'

Matt looks at her and his piercing blue eyes seem to melt with warmth.

'It 'as me. I've not been able to think of owt else since I saw yer.'

'Nor me.'

'I don't do affairs. Waste of time. And yet 'ere we are.'

'This isn't an affair, we're just having lunch.' says Julia, matter of-factly.

'It is an affair inside me 'ead, Gigi. And me 'eart.' Matt looks at Julia pointedly. 'And everywhere else.'

'What does that mean?' asks Julia, looking into his eyes then down at her glass, where she's running her forefinger along the rim as though she's waiting for it to make a ringing sound. She glances back up at him, shyly.

'Stop playin' games wi' me. Yer know what it means.' he says, gently.

'Yes, I do, I'm sorry. I...I just keep trying to convince myself that this is nothing more than an attractive young man wanting to do a bit of...wolfing around.'

'*Wolfing around?*' Matt bursts out laughing.

Giano sails towards them holding a silver ice bucket containing a bottle of wine, a folded napkin over the other arm. He places the wine cooler on the table, uncorks the bottle and, with one arm behind his back, and stooping slightly, proceeds to pour a little wine into Julia's glass.

'I hope you like. This is a beautiful wine, a great choice by *Signor Matt*. He has, as always, such impeccable taste, in wine as, on this occasion, his taste in company.' He smiles fondly at Julia, who, for the first time since entering the restaurant, blushes.

'You're wonderfully charming.' she says with a smile to Giano. 'I wish English men were like Italians, I love them.'

'We love that you love us!' he exclaims, grinning from ear to ear. 'This is why we make you such wonderful food! You love our country, we make sure you love our food!'

Julia takes a sip of the wine and smiles, 'It's gorgeous, thank you.'

Giano tops up her glass before filling Matt's and smiles from one to the other. 'Are you ready to order or do you need more time?'

'I'm so sorry, I've not even looked at the menu yet, hold on, I'll do it now.' says Julia, opening the lunch menu and quickly scanning it.

'I'll have the tris di crostini followed by the tagliatelli alla campagnola, please Giano.' says Matt, confidently.

'That looks great. Me too.' says Julia, decisively.

'*Perfecto!*' Giano smiles again, bows slightly and floats back towards the kitchen.

Julia looks at Matt with a level expression. 'Look, I'm older than your mother. I don't have a perfect body, I've had a baby,

I'm going through the menopause, the girls you're used to, they have flat stomachs and a gap between their thighs, they won't have saggy *flaps* at the top of their arms.'

'Bingo wings.'

'Cheers.'

'No problem.'

'What I'm trying to say, Matt, is that all girls are beautiful and perfect at your age. Age has ruined me, I'm like a rose that's blown over...'

Matt leans slightly forward and reaches out for Julia's hand, which is nervously wringing her napkin. He clasps her hand in his and looks into her eyes.

'Bollocks' he whispers, then adds, before she can respond, 'Gigi, I've fallen in love with you.'

Julia takes a deep breath, her heart feels as though it has turned to stone and is now struggling to beat inside her.

'Matt...oh god...I feel the same. I've fallen in love with you too. Which is *completely insane.*'

'No, it isn't. There's nothing insane about it, Gigi, we're just two people who've met and are spiritually totally on the same wave length. Your body doesn't come into it. Although you do have fantastic breasts...' his eyes light up, mischievously.

'It's nice. That you say that. Without it sounding lecherous...'

'Gigi...I feel I should be honest with you. Yer know I said I was a plumber?'

'Yes...'

'Well I'm not a plumber.' says Matt, smiling. 'Although I can fix owt...'

'Really? So what do you do then?'

'I'm a model. When I met you I was off for a fitting at Stella McCartney's.' Matt takes a swig of his wine, grins and picks up a bread roll, which he tears in half with his fingers before spreading with butter.

❧❧❧

Within a split second, Matt is in the centre of a dizzying vortex and the rest of the world around him is just a whizzing blur. Julia's stomach is filled with a rock so heavy it threatens to plummet through her bowels and drag her beneath the ground along with it. Her head feels light and dizzy, she can barely focus. How many stunningly beautiful male models with blonde curly hair, as Kate has already described him, called 'Matt' are there living in Hemel Hempstead? Fuck. Fuck fuck fuck fuck *fuck*. She is sitting there in front of her daughter's boyfriend. Again. This cannot be happening. Life just doesn't throw up coincidences this extreme.

'Are you alright, luv?' asks Matt, nonchalantly. 'You look a bit pale. Not shocked you, have I? Doesn't mean I'm gay, just coz I'm a model.'

'I'm fine. I'm absolutely fine.' she replies in a monotone, obviously not fine at all.

Julia stares at her glass of wine, her mind teeming with thoughts.

'Fuck, and I was about to come clean and tell him my real name. I can't do that now. How many Julia and Alex's live in Tewin? I'm *not* giving this up.' thinks Julia to herself. 'I don't care who he is, I deserve this, you only live once and I am not giving this up. Gigi I will stay, for now...'

Matt continues with the big reveal about his life whilst Julia gazes at him in stunned silence.

'So I'm surrounded by drop-dead beautiful girls all day. More beautiful than you can imagine. Some of these girls are like oil paintings once they've got their slap and kit on. But then you'll see one backstage, sitting there on a stool, looking like a Greek sculpture, just radiating pure beauty, and she lights up a fag and says 'Oooh have you seen what's happened in *Corrie?* I couldn't *believe* it, it was like *soooo* random!' and you realise you're fucking *miles* apart.' Matt squeezes Julia's hand. 'It's not about looks and age, Gigi, it's about *soul*.'

'Oh Matt...' Looking at him and hearing his voice, her shock melts away and Julia is suddenly filled with a surge of longing.

Matt looks at her levelly again. 'I want to fuck you. I've thought about nothing else ever since I met you outside the gallery.'

'I *want* you to fuck me. To make love to me. When?' Julia scans Matt's eyes and feels as though she's fallen into a deep pool from which she'll never escape, nor wants to.

'Soon. Let's book a hotel.'

'I can be in London again tomorrow night. I'll say I'm up here again to see a friend. Livia. She's a children's book author. Sometimes I stay over with her.'

'I'll be free.'

Giano approaches from their periphery vision, bearing plates of steaming hot food with a big smile on his face. Lunch. Julia feels as though lunch at Stef's is going to be etched on her memory for as long as she lives.

15

MOTHER, YOU'LL NEVER BELIEVE THIS...

don't even care if she's seeing Matt, fuck him, he's boring and I'm not even in love with him, Mum's welcome to him, he's an idiot who wouldn't even take me to the Matthew Williamson show, wanker. But I'm telling her about Alex and that complete *tramp*.' thinks Kate.

❧❧❧

In the taxi from Welwyn Garden City to Tewin, Julia's mobile rings. It's Kate. Julia's heart lurches and she feels sick. Has Kate found out? Already? This is crazy.

Julia: Hello darling...
Kate: *Mother!* You will never fucking believe this...

Phew. She doesn't know. But why would she?

Julia: What?
Kate: You sound edgy and nervous. What's wrong? Has that twat said anything?
Julia: What twat?
Kate: *Alex!* Your boyfriend! My *ex-husband!* There's only one twat, Mother! Actually there's two twats but never you mind

about *that*. Make that *three*. In fact *everyone in my life* is a fucking twat right now.

Julia: I don't know what you're talking about but in answer to your question, no, I haven't seen him for a couple of days. He's come home late two nights on the trot and left before I've got up.

Kate: Oh. Well *that* fits. Cunt.

Julia: What's he done? Tell me!

Kate: Well. I went to see him at the agency the day before yesterday...

Julia: Why?

Kate: Just something, OK? You don't need to know what. Just something I fucking needed to sort out OK?

Julia: OK...

Kate:...and he was *all over* this woman at work.

Julia inwardly feels a massive surge of relief. 'Thank fuck for that. My pass to guilt-free fucking Matt. Apart from my daughter. Fuck!'

Julia: Really? What did she look like?

Kate: A slut. Tarty. Last season's wardrobe. Fake tits. Blonde.

Julia: Classy.

Kate: She was running her hands all over him, Mum. There is obviously something going on between them. What is he like? He can't keep it in his pants! He is such a fucking tosser. I don't know why you haven't seen through him by now. You know what, Mum, since Dad died, your taste in men has gone completely *to shit*.

Julia: That's not fair, Kate! You loved Alex at one time as well!

Kate: Not properly. I never really loved him, he was always a twat. Once a tosser, always a twat.

Julia: Well yes, that makes sense.

Kate: *Nothing* makes sense!

Kate's voice is rising with anger now. Julia can hear a slurping noise in between sentences.

Julia: Are you drinking, darling? It's not even five o'clock.

Kate: Yes I fucking am, and so what? I'm going through *hell* here Mother, you have no idea!

Julia: Why should it matter to you that Alex is flirting with some bimbo at work? Surely that's *my* concern...

Kate: Because he was a wanker going off with you and now he's being a wanker again.

Julia: I can handle it, Kate, don't go getting upset about this.

Kate: Well *somebody* should be upset because *you* don't sound very fucking upset *Mother*...why aren't you bothered? Has it all gone *wrong?*

Julia doesn't like the tone creeping into Kate's voice, the sarcasm has a strange nasty edge to it now.

Julia: Look, it's not great, OK? We have been having problems...

Kate: What, like the fact you're old enough to be his *mother? Those* kind of problems?

Julia: Don't get nasty with me or I'm hanging up, Kate.

Kate: I *feel* nasty. I feel fucking angry and pissed off with the lot of you!

Julia: What 'lot' of us?

Kate: You, that cunt Alex, that cunt Matt, and you're not behaving like a proper mother and haven't since you went through this mid-life crisis and started shagging *babies.*

Julia: *One* baby...and he's not a *baby.* He's *thirty-one.* That's a grown man.

Kate: He's a ridiculous spoilt *child* and you totally *indulge* him.

Julia: No, I don't. Look Kate, how many times do we have to have this conversation? We've been going round in circles for the last eighteen months. I fell in love with your husband, it was a crazy thing to happen but it's a crazy world and crazy shit happens. And you were, let's not forget, desperately unhappy with him and still seeing your ex behind Alex's back. So I hardly ruined a beautiful relationship. I picked up a few of the smashed pieces to make something else.

Kate: Out of *my husband*, Mother!

Julia: I'm sorry Kate, I'm sorry for the way it happened. Neither of us chose it to happen this way, it just did.

Kate: Well I'm sorry too. I'm sorry I had to stand there and watch that primal *ape* groping that *slut* right in front of me. She won't be the first you know. I bet he's shagged half the fucking agency.

Julia: Look darling, my taxi's just got home, I have to pay him. I'll ring you back later.

Kate: Where have you been?

Julia: I've been to lunch in London. With Livia.

Kate: Really. Well I hope you enjoyed yourselves. Funny, because Matt's in London today. He said he was going to lunch with some art director.

Julia: Well, there are a couple of million people in London so it's hardly surprising we both know someone who was there today.

Kate: Nothing would surprise me now. Fucking *nothing*. Bye, Mother.

Kate has hung up the phone before Julia has a chance to reply. Very odd. Why was she so angry? Is she just doing the usual Kate thing, trying to cause trouble? She's certainly managed to burst the beautiful bubble in which Julia had been floating all day, prior to meeting Matt, over lunch at Stef's, the deep, passionate kiss outside Stef's on the pavement and then sitting on the train alone, day-dreaming about fucking Matt all the way home.

She stands on the threshold of her house, the key half in the lock, wondering what to do about this. She needs some evidence. This is going to be her excuse for fucking Matt.

❦ ❦ ❦

Julia pours herself a glass of wine and walks into the study. Alex's laptop is on the computer table, which is unusual as normally he takes it to work with him. She opens it up and types in one of his usual passwords to get into his account. It doesn't work so she tries another one of his regular passwords. Bingo.

Sunrise calendar...that's the one. Julia opens it up and scrolls through the next few days. Every day and every evening he's got meetings scheduled with some 'Sandi' on the Jaffa Cake account. That must be her, then. He's mentioned Jaffa Cakes before but hadn't told her he was working closely with anyone else on it. The little shit. Julia takes a large swig of her wine, gets out her iPhone and rings Alex.

Julia: Hi. I....I thought I'd touch base with you Alex, because I haven't seen you for literally days on end. What's going on?

Alex: I've been busy. You know I have. I left you a note yesterday and the day before saying I was leaving early for work and I've been working late, too. You haven't bothered to ring me to talk to me, even.

Julia: Well to be honest, Alex, I was rather put out by the fact that you've only been coming home to sleep these past couple of days. What have you been working on that's so important?

Alex: The Jaffa Cake site. I told you. The client's moved the deadline forward and now wants a coded preview by the end of the week. It's incredibly stressful, Julia.

123

Julia: So, are you working on this alone? Or have you got a colleague to help you?

Alex: I'm...well...yes, a colleague. Look I'm actually really busy right now Julia, can't we discuss this at a later date?

Julia: Oh so I need to book a date in order to find out why my boyfriend is never at home now, do I?

Alex: (whispering into the phone) Look, Julia, this is an open plan office, people can hear you talking.

Julia: Well *go the fuck outside then.*

Alex: I don't know why you're being so difficult, Julia, I really don't.

Julia: What's the name of the colleague?

Alex: Why? What on earth does it matter? What are you asking me *that* for?

Julia: So it's a woman. Well, that's established that one, anyway. What's her name?

Alex: Look, I'm not going to be the subject of an interrogation when I'm busy at work.

Julia: Is she there now? Is she listening? What does she look like? Oh hold on, let me guess. Twenty-something, tall, leggy, blonde, big breasts.

Alex: (hissing) You are being fucking ridiculous, Julia.

Julia: So I'm right. What's her name?

Alex: I'm not doing this right here.

Julia: Right. She's standing next to you, listening. What is her fucking name, Alex?

Alex: (sarcastically) My colleague is called Sandi and she's a brilliant designer. Would you like to say hello to her? I can pass the phone over if you like.

Julia: No thank you, Darling. I'm sure she's a brilliant designer. So, when are you planning to fuck her? Or have you fucked her already? You certainly aren't bothering to fuck me nowadays.

Alex: That's something we need to discuss privately.

Julia: I wonder what she thinks you're talking about.

Alex: Tell her! Go on! Here!

Julia: (hissing as well) *Don't you fucking dare pass me onto her.* I don't trust you, Alex Harcourt. I don't believe you and I don't trust you. But you know what? *I don't fucking care.* Go ahead and shag your bimbo design assistant if you want to. See if I care. Because I don't. I couldn't give two shits. You're pathetically transparent, you know that? You're not even a very good liar. You betrayed my daughter and now you're betraying *me.*

Alex: Really. Well you should know about betrayal, Julia, because according to Kate, you were sucking face with *her boyfriend*, that *model*, at the National Portrait Gallery two days ago!

Julia: What? That is ridiculous. Where did Kate get such a crazy idea from?

Alex: Well apparently, Julia, Kate actually *saw* you. She turned up at work wearing a ridiculous disguise, a blonde wig and hippie clothes, and said she'd just come from the NPG where she'd caught you and Matt or whatever he's called, swapping saliva in the middle of a bunch of Grace Coddingtons.

Julia: I wasn't even *at* the National Portrait Gallery on Monday! I don't know where Kate's got this idea from but she's obviously mixed me up with someone else. Anyway, her boyfriend's even younger than you, he's twenty-five or something isn't he? Do you really think I'd make the same mistake I made with you and go for someone even younger? Hmmm? Twenty-five is a *child*, Alex, you're being ridiculous.

Alex: Do you know what, Julia? Sometimes I think you and Kate are as bad and mad as each other. Her turning up at work dressed like that and causing a scene, and you...how could she mistake two complete strangers for her own mother and her boyfriend? Unless she's completely lost the plot...

Julia: I'll talk to her. Everything's getting out of hand, Alex. If you spent more time at home and less time at work, none of this would be happening.

Alex: So it's my fault.

Julia: Basically, yes.

Alex: Look, I'm in the corridor, I have to get back into the office, we're in the middle of something.

Julia: You are indeed, Alex, you are indeed...

16

CHRISTINA

hey are all full of shit. All of them. My mother, who 's got this pathetic obsession with men young enough to be her own kids. Matt who's turned out to be a typical shallow model completely up his own arse, and my ex-husband Alex who is no more than a drooling primate. Fuck the lot of them! The only two decent people in my life now are Tanya and Colin! I need to get out of this pathetic nest of vipers and expand my horizons a bit. I know people! I'm popular! That photographer I met at Matthew Williamson's, whatsername, Christina, she said she'd like to meet up with me for a drink. Yeah, fuck I should give her a ring! Fuck Matt, Alex and my completely crazy mother, fuck them all, they can all fuck off!

৵৻৵৻৵৻

Kate arrives five minutes late at The Crown and Two Chairmen in Dean Street. She's wearing cork platform sandals and a skin-tight pink and yellow dress in a pattern of swirling florals. She walks into the dimly lit interior where a few media types are sitting eating at one of the big wooden tables near the window.

A bearded young man in aviator shades with huge reflective yellow lenses is talking animatedly, his fork hovering in mid-air with a morsel of food perched on the end of it. He's accompanied by two women in their twenties, both impossibly thin, dressed in scarves and streamlined dresses, their noses turned up in the air, studiously ignoring everyone else in the pub except their own tight-knit little group.

A woman in jeans and a band t-shirt bearing the words 'Venus Tree' is sitting at the bar drinking a glass of white wine and chatting to the barmaid. Kate looks towards the seating in the corner, to her right, and there is Christina. She's tall with long brunette hair, partly swept up into a beehive, the rest of her hair draped languidly around her shoulders. She's wearing black cargo pants and a black exercise top exposing her perfectly flat stomach. Unlike the snotty media chicks, Christina is interestedly observing everyone around her. She's hispanic looking, stunningly beautiful with full lips, a small, perfectly formed, aquiline nose and huge almond-shaped brown eyes – she could be the double of Penelope Cruz.

She smiles a broad, warm smile as Kate notices her and stands up to greet her, hugging and kissing her on both cheeks.

Christina: Hi darling. You look amazing! Where did you get that dress?

Kate glances round conspiratorially. She murmurs,

Kate: Primani...
Christina: Hahaha you're so funny, Kate.

Kate points to Christina's top.

Kate: Nice. What does 'Kurokuma' mean?
Christina: Black bear. Apparently.
Kate: Who are they?
Christina: Doom band. From Sheffield.

Christina

Kate: You know so much about music. You've heard of all the cool underground stuff!

Christina smiles, seductively.

Christina: I get around, darling. What do you want to drink?
Kate: I'll have a gin and tonic, plenty of ice, please.
Christina: Be right back.

Kate follows Christina to the bar with her eyes, and realises in an instant that she's rarely seen such a beautiful woman in the flesh. Christina leans easily against the bar, chatting with the barmaid and smiling. Now she's laughing, a big, wide, open laugh, her eyes crinkling in the corners. She reaches across herself and adjusts her bra strap, glancing over to Kate as she does so and catches Kate watching her. She winks and grins. Unusual. Kate hasn't been winked at for a very long time.

Christina returns with the drinks and puts them on the table in front of Kate.

Christina: Love this pub.
Kate: Apart from the media types.
Christina: Sweetie, I *am* a media type!
Kate: (glancing across at the three people across the room, now hunched over talking earnestly to one another.) Not like *them* you're not.
Christina: No, I guess not. So, what's been going on in your life? It was so nice meeting you at Matt Williamson's party. I get bored talking to the same people every place I go to.
Kate: Actually, a lot's been going on. A fuck of a lot. I've discovered that my entire family are total wankers.
Christina: Why?

Kate: Well, I didn't tell you at Matt's, but my mother is shacked up with my ex-husband, Alex. In my old family home in Tewin. It's just a total *sacrilege*.

Christina: *No way!*

Kate: *Way.* They started seeing another whilst I was married to him. I mean, I didn't actually care that much because I was still seeing my ex, Colin, who's lovely. But the thought of your own mother having sex is so completely *ew* anyway, and the thought of her having sex with your husband is just beyond gross.

Christina: Too *right!* Oh, you poor baby!

Kate: And now…she's started seeing my fucking *boyfriend!* I caught them snogging at the National Portrait Gallery the other day. You couldn't make it up. If you read it in a book you'd think it was too outlandish to believe.

Christina: *Fuck.* Oh Kate, darling, that is *awful.*

Kate: And as if that wasn't bad enough, I've just found out that Alex is now sniffing around this utter *skank* he works with behind my mum's back! I mean, yeah, my mum is living with my ex-husband and about to shag my current boyfriend but she's still *my mum!* I still *care* about her!

Christina: *Babes!*

Kate takes a large swig of her gin and tonic and shakes her head in disbelief.

Kate: Office slut is such a *tramp.* Right piece of work. Who'd have thought it? Boring old Alex Harcourt is now a *serial shagger.*

Christina: You've been through a hard time, darling, haven't you?

Kate: It's been shit. You can't trust anyone.

Christina puts her drink down, reaches over and strokes Kate's hair, gently, looking into her eyes.

Christina: Well any man who chooses another woman over you is insane, Kate. You're beautiful. And sensuous. Pearls before swine.

Kate blinks rapidly and smiles across at Christina, holding her gaze. She glances down at Christina's full, pink lips and her heart starts beating fast. Suddenly she realises how gorgeous Christina is. Kate's never been excited by a woman before, never mind slept with one. But Christina is something else. She looks back up at Christina's eyes and Christina is still looking at her intently, her brown eyes almost melting with affection and desire.

Kate's lips involuntarily part slightly. Christina reaches out and gently runs her index finger across the top of Kate's upper lip, then brushes it against the skin of her lower lip, before gently inserting the tip of her finger into Kate's mouth. Kate licks and then sucks Christina's finger, never taking her eyes from Christina's, even for a moment. She feels as though she's going to melt into a puddle on the floor.

Christina pulls her finger from Kate's mouth and Kate reaches out and cups Christina's face between her hands, before moving towards her and kissing her on the mouth. Christina's lips part and as Kate feels Christina's gentle, sensuous tongue on hers she feels as though her heart is going to burst. Christina pulls Kate towards her and now Kate can feel Christina's breasts against hers and feels unbearably aroused. They kiss deeply for a while before pulling away from one another, still looking into one another's eyes.

Christina: Let's go back to mine and make love, Kate. Would you like that?

Kate can barely breathe, but whispers 'Yes.'

❧❧❧

Kate and Christina stand silently next to each other on the busy tube to Aldgate East, their secret buried deep between them. Kate knows virtually nothing about this new friend, she's a fashion photographer who seemed, when they met, to know everyone in the business. So she's obviously well-liked and respected. And so beautiful. She should be a model herself. Christina glances across at Kate and a faint smile passes over her lips.

'I don't even know what to do...' thinks Kate. 'What do women *do* in bed? How do they make love? I've got no idea...'

Christina seems to read Kate's thoughts because she covertly reaches out and squeezes Kate's hand, her thoughtful, pursed-lipped pout broadening to a wide smile, her eyes lighting up with delight and mischief.

From the tube, the pair walk up Brick Lane then turn right half way up, down Heneage Street. A few locals are standing outside The Pride of Spitalfields pub, drinking in the warmth of the balmy evening.

'It's down here, on the left' says Christina, indicating a row of Victorian terraced houses.

'Wow, so cool that you live here! It's in the middle of everything!' coos Kate, admiringly.

'It was my grandfather's house, been in the family for years. My parents had it converted into flats, I've got the top floor and the rest is rented...'

Christina puts the key in the lock and opens the front door. An automatic light illuminates a bright, white hallway from which other doors lead. Christina leads Kate up two flights of stairs until finally they reach the top floor. The door opens onto a dimly-lit room crammed with photography gear. Stacks of boxes, photography cases, tripods and piles of papers surround a state of the art Apple Mac on a large wooden table underneath a velux window with the blind drawn shut, giving the room an air of neglect and gloom.

'This is my work room. Apologies for the mess.' laughs Christina, before pushing open another door which leads into a cool, white, spacious bedroom with a large dormer window overlooking Heneage Street.

Christina casually saunters by an iPod docking station and puts music on, the soothing sounds of old-school Ibiza grooves filling the room with honeyed notes.

In the middle of the room is a large bed covered in a white duvet, with a small fridge next to it. Christina opens the fridge and casually produces a bottle of cava and two chilled wine glasses.

'Hold on, I've got some olives, too...' she says airily, before wandering off through an adjoining door and returning with a silver Moroccan tray covered in plump olives, swimming in oil.

Kate has never met anyone before so effortlessly brimming with poise, calm and confidence. Christina is like something out of a glossy magazine advert, an other-worldly goddess.

Kate wanders over to the window and looks down at the street below.

'I guess...you do this, kind of, a lot, then?'

Christina opens the bottle of cava, smiling, and pours them each a glass.

'Nope. I spend most of my time working. I'm too knackered for relationships. Besides...'

'What?'

Christina hands Kate a glass of cava and proffers her own glass to chink cheers.

'Cheers...so glad you're here, this is nice.' smiles Christina.

'Cheers...yes, it's lovely...I like your place.' smiles Kate. 'So, you were saying...besides what?'

'I was engaged. About four years ago. He fucked off with this solicitor...I haven't...I can't...I've not wanted to get involved since. I prefer female company now. Not because of him...he was never enough, if I'm honest. He was childish. Crazy about football. Expected me to do all the cooking. I'm not going *there* again. So now, I have girlfriends. Well, one or two...I find women much easier company, to be frank.'

'Yeah.' says Kate, sighing, and, to her horror, feels tears welling up in her eyes.

Christina puts her glass down and walks over to the window. She touches Kate's shoulder, gently. 'It's a man's world. And most of them are stupid. We have to make whatever we can of it.'

Kate puts her own glass down on the windowsill and wraps her arms around Christina, pulling her towards her. They stand, holding one another - the bond already forming between them feels greater than something based on mere animal function. Kate looks up at Christina and brushes a strand of dark hair away from her face. Christina kisses Kate and sinks into the tender warmth of her mouth. They stand there in the glow of the afternoon sunlight from the window, kissing gently, for what seems like an eternity. Then Christina runs her hands down Kate's back and over her slight hips, curving the palm of her hands around Kate's bottom. Kate pushes her body towards Christina's so that she's pressed hard against her. She longs to touch Christina's full, firm breasts, but daren't, nervous and unsure in this new and unexplored territory.

Christina pulls away from their kiss, smiles gently at Kate and takes her hand, leading her over to the bed, with its white duvet, white pillowcases and a floppy pink and white plush toy cat incongruously lying at an angle on one of the pillows.

Christina stands by the bed and pulls her black vest over her head, revealing a red satin bra and large, round breasts, the edge of which protrude slightly over the top of her bra as though it's holding them tight, lest they escape. She reaches back, unfastens her bra and takes it off. Her breasts, full, with small, brown pert nipples, sticking out invitingly, seem to breathe a sigh of relief at being free.

Kate can barely catch her breath. She's never seen anything so beautiful.

Christina is smiling at her and now Kate has the courage to reach out and touch Christina's breasts. She places one hand on each soft, warm breast and caresses them, sighing deeply, rubbing her fingers over the nipples, which tighten even further with excitement.

'Take your dress off' murmurs Christina, gently, and reaches down to remove her cargo pants, then moves her hand down towards her satin knickers which stretch tightly against her perfectly flat stomach, slipping her fingers under the top of them and sliding them down her legs, all the while smiling at Kate seductively and mischievously.

Kate has stopped feeling so shy now, she confidently unhooks the back of her dress and pulls it quickly over her head, instantly revealing her small, perfectly formed breasts. She slips her white knickers down her legs and now both women stand naked, facing one another.

Christina moves towards the bed and lies down, reaching out her hand for Kate to join her. Kate lies down next to her and smiles.

'You're so beautiful, Christina.'

'So are you.'

'Matt never tells me I'm beautiful.'

'Well he's an idiot.' Christina almost whispers.

Christina leans on one arm with her head in her palm, and runs her other hand languidly over Kate's body, caressing her breasts, massaging her taut stomach and then moving her hand down to the triangle of hair on Kate's pubis. She slips her thumb down in the crack between Kate's legs and gently strokes the folds of skin of Kate's pussy. Kate sighs and parts her legs slightly, feeling herself become instantly wet and unbearably aroused.

In turn, Kate caresses Christina, propped up on one arm facing her, mirroring Christina's body, running her hands across Christina's breasts, marvelling at how large and firm they are. Kate has never felt another woman's breasts before and can't believe how sensuous they feel after the flat hardness of a man's chest. She caresses each mound, cupping one after the other in turn and feeling its weight, running her fingers across each firm, pointed brown nipple. Then she moves down to Christina's thick bush of pubic hair, dark, curly and un-trimmed. Like Christina herself, it looks luxuriantly defiant in its refusal to be tamed and Kate longs to explore it. She pushes two fingers between Christina's legs and Christina gasps with pleasure as Kate gently slides her fingers over the already slippery folds of flesh of Christina's pussy.

'I don't know what I'm doing. I've never done this before.' whispers Kate.

'It's beautiful. You're beautiful.' sighs Christina.

'Do you like the way I'm touching you?'

'Yes....I'd love to feel your mouth against me though.'

Kate smiles, grateful to be guided, even though everything seems so beautiful and so natural.

Christina rolls on to her back. Kate slides down the bed as Christina parts her legs, revealing the soft folds of her pussy, glistening with oily arousal. Kate lies between Christina's legs and props her arms on her elbows. She brushes one hand through the soft bush of Christina's pubic hair then places the flat of her palms on Christina's stomach. She bends down and pushes her face into the soft fleshy folds of Christina's pussy and sighs, heavily, feeling overwhelmed by the heady scent of ocean pearls embracing her nose and lips, which she parts, to run her tongue across Christina's soft skin. She makes a slow, almost chewing motion as she manipulates the folds of Christina's skin with her mouth and tongue and Christina sighs, heavily,

'God, that's beautiful, Kate. And you say you've never done this before?'

'Mmmmn' Kate can't talk, lost as she is in the beautiful scents and contours of Christina's vulva.

Kate slips her hand down between her own legs and starts caressing herself, masturbating as she licks, nibbles and chews Christina's pussy. She finds a steady rhythm, in time with her own fingers pulsating back and forth over her clitoris, and moves her lips and tongue rhythmically over Christina's clitoris and the folds of skin covering it.

Christina throws her head back into the pillow, lost in ecstasy, gently running her hands through Kate's hair, her full lips parted with sighs.

Kate can feel the heat in Christina's pussy under her tongue and senses that she's going to come at any second. It's too much. She can't hold off her own orgasm any longer. She stretches her legs as wide as they will go in anticipation and comes in an explosion of ecstasy, moaning as she continues to suck and tease and lick Christina, whose bottom raises up off the bed in an electric shock of orgasm, so that Kate has to hold her hips to maintain contact as Christina's body throbs back and forth in ecstasy.

Christina sinks back into the bed and Kate moves her mouth away from the heat of her pussy, resting her lips on the top of Christina's thighs and kissing her skin, gently.

Christina gently pulls Kate's shoulders and Kate looks up. Christina is looking at her with a deep look of love and pulls Kate up the bed until they are lying facing one another again. They fall into one another's arms and kiss deeply, each running their hands over the other's body, insatiable with lust. Christina reaches out and pulls the pink and white cat towards her. She unzips the bottom of the toy and produces a large dildo, sculpted to look like a penis. It's huge, Kate gasps and can't help thinking that it's bigger than either Alex or Matt when they're erect. She likes it.

Christina gazes at Kate seductively and, lying on her back, puts the dildo against her vulva. rubbing it softly against her clitoris.

'Push it into me, Kate.' she says thickly. 'Please.'

Kate takes the dildo, places the tip against Christina's vulva and pushes gently. It slides easily in, all the way up to the base, so slippery is Christina after her orgasm. Christina moans with pleasure.

Kate smiles and leans down, taking one of Christina's nipples into her mouth and sucking it gently as she withdraws the dildo all the way before gently plunging it back into the depths of Christina's vagina. Christina slides her hand down towards her vulva and starts masturbating as Kate fucks her slowly with the dildo, moaning and gasping with pleasure. She comes again in seconds, her body arching and thrashing, Kate continuing to push the dildo in and out until Christina grasps it to stop its motion, collapsing back onto the bed, completely spent and exhausted.

After a few minutes of repose and fulfilment, Christina slowly opens her eyes and looks at Kate, who is propped up on one arm, smiling with joy.

'Now it's your turn.' she whispers.

17

AT THE IBIS, COMMERCIAL ROAD

 ying on her back, the sheets tousled beneath her body and staring at the ceiling as Christina dozes peacefully beside her, her arm draped across Kate's body, Kate realises that she hasn't felt this happy in a long time. She turns her head to look out of the window.

Just outside, a magpie is chattering noisily. Suddenly it drops down from the roof, swoops past Christina's bedroom window and back up again, flapping over the rooftops of Brick Lane, across Wentworth Street and over towards Commercial Street where it swoops down, almost to street level, and lands on top of the awning of the Ibis London City hotel's lounge windows.

Inside the hotel lounge, Kate's mother is leaning forward in her chair to pick up a glass of red wine from the little round table in front of her.

Julia shifts in her seat, nervously, arranging the folds of her full-length, cotton summer dress around her legs. She feels electrified with excitement at the thought that any minute now, one of the most gorgeous men she has ever set eyes on is about to walk into the hotel lounge and take her upstairs to make love to her.

The wine relaxes her slightly and she looks up. Above her are huge, white, spherical lampshades which glow reassuringly. The decor is 1960s *Mad Men*, minimalist, swish and retro, nothing like the plush, polished wood and glossed leather lounges of so many hotels in years gone by, hangovers of a long-gone Victorian era. Now everything feels spacious, light and airy.

As Julia looks around at the various arrangements of seats around tables, the brick wall facing the lounge area and the smart, modern bar beyond, she wonders how many stories play themselves out here day in, day out. Lovers, lies, secrets, excitement, boredom, duty, loneliness, love and lust. All under one roof.

⅔⅔⅔

Matt emerges from Aldgate East tube station feeling hot, sweaty and tired after a wasted day of go sees that didn't actually go anywhere. His iPhone pings.

i'm here. waiting in lounge. x

He stops to text back.

almost there x

He's just round the corner from the Ibis. He can't remember ever wanting a woman as much as he wants Gigi right now. There is something fundamentally out of reach about her. She's unobtainable in a way that younger women aren't. And yet she's about thirty seconds away from him now, sitting there, waiting for him. A pang of guilt shoots through his stomach. Kate hasn't done anything to deserve this betrayal. Matt knows that she's still been knocking around with that Colin bloke, but is pretty sure they haven't been sleeping together. But he's living with Kate. This is going to make things difficult. Maybe he should just turn around and go back to the tube station. This is pure deception. He wasn't planning a full-blown affair. And yet it's not just that he wants Gigi. He has to have her.

The door to the Ibis is there in front of him. Julia is beyond it, waiting for him.

Fuck it.

She sees him walking towards her. He's wearing jeans, cowboy boots and a white t-shirt. He looks as if he's just stepped down from an advertising hoarding. He is gorgeous. As usual. He pushes his shades up so they rest in his thick, curly blonde hair and grins.

Julia knocks back the last drop of wine in her glass, stands up and they hug one another, warmly. Julia breathes a huge sigh of relief, that he's here, that she's with him.

'You look gorgeous.' says Matt, smiling, before kissing Julia softly on the mouth in greeting.

Julia's legs feel as though they're about to give way under her, she feels completely out of control, as though he's already inside her and she inside him. He smells faintly of lavender and fresh sweat. She wants him now, she doesn't even want to wait until they get to their room.

Matt catches the way she's looking at him and smiles, before taking her hand and walking with her to the reception desk.

At the reception desk stands a strikingly beautiful Indian girl of about Matt's age, with long black hair wound up into an elegant *chignon*, heavy make-up and wearing a crisply pressed white shirt and grey skirt-suit.

Matt hands her the print-off of his reservation and she quickly types into the computer in front of her. 'Breakfast is served between 4am and 11am and you have a choice of Continental or Traditional English. Enjoy your stay.' she says smiling, handing Julia the key card.

Their room is on the seventh floor. The second they step into the lift, they fall on one another and start kissing, passionately.

Matt holds Julia close to him and runs his hands down over her bottom, through the thin cotton fabric of her dress. Julia pushes her hands under his t-shirt to feel his skin, warm, taut, smooth and muscled...still she feels as though she's going to collapse with excitement, joy and sheer desire for him.

They lift draws to a halt at their floor and they emerge into the corridor. Their room is the first one to the right. They smile at one another and Matt slips the key card into its slot, turns the handle and opens the door.

Julia walks in first, followed by Matt who closes the door behind him. They immediately fall into one another's arms and kiss deeply again. Matt pulls Julia's dress up and she takes over and pulls it over her head, dropping it to the floor. She walks towards the bed in her bra and knickers then quickly slips them off before lying naked on the bed. She stretches out, languorously, then reaches up and strokes her own breasts as she looks at Matt, who smiles and sighs with contentment, watching her as he removes his t-shirt, then sits down next to her on the bed, takes off his cowboy boots and throws them one by one across the floor before standing up again, unbuckling his belt and pulling off his jeans.

He's standing there in front of her now in just his pants, through which Julia can see his stiff erection pressing against the fabric. He grins as he peels them off slowly and they drop to the floor. His penis is huge, jutting out in front of his body and arching upwards. He lies down next to her and they hold one another and Julia sighs as she buries her face into Matt's neck,

'God, you are absolutely beautiful.' She pulls away and looks into his eyes and runs her fingers through his blonde, curly hair. 'I want you so much.' she murmurs.

'I want you, Gigi.' Matt runs his hands over Julia's breasts, feeling the curve and weight of them. 'Your breasts are beautiful.

You're beautiful. Oh god Gigi, I've never wanted to fuck a woman as much as I want to fuck you right now...'

Julia reaches down and holds his penis in her hand, running her hand gently up and down the shaft, rubbing her thumb over the already glistening head which is swollen and red with excitement. Then she moves her hands onto his back and runs her hands over his shoulders and down his back, before pulling him towards and on top of her.

'I can't wait. Fuck me now.' she whispers. He kisses her deeply on the mouth as she guides his penis into her. He pushes down with one long thrust and Julia pulls away from their kiss and gasps out loud as he fills her. 'Oh god, Matt.' He immediately starts pumping into her with long, hard thrusts of his penis, she raises her legs to ease his access and moans as she feels heat rising from deep within her groin.

Matt lifts himself up on his elbows so that he can see Julia's body. Every time he thrusts into her, her large breasts tremble, the nipples now hard and pert, wobbling with the rhythm of his thrusting. He's never fucked a woman with such large breasts before and the excitement of watching their undulating movement as the warmth of her vagina embraces his penis in its slick oiliness, is almost too much to bear.

He pumps into her harder and harder and Julia cries out as the wave of heat inside her rushes up through her entire body in a sudden orgasm. Julia's head lolls back in ecstasy and her eyes become unfocused and half closed, her lips parted as she moans and gasps.

The flow of warm fluid into her pussy surrounding his cock overwhelms him and with a few more thrusts he explodes inside her, pumping out what feels like an ocean of spunk in thick, long spurts before slowly sinking down onto her body, completely spent.

Julia rubs her hands through his hair, down his back, cups his buttocks in her hands and runs her hands back up to his shoulders where they rest, holding him close.

Matt buries his face in Julia's long, wavy hair and drinks in her scent before moving to look at her. He looks into her eyes and she smiles.

'Fuck. Gigi.'

'Fuck. Matt. Fuck. Oh god'

'That was amazing.'

'I know.'

'This isn't normal, Gigi. God, I came so quickly, I'm sorry.'

'It's fine. We have all evening and all night.' whispers Julia. 'That was amazing.'

Matt looks at Julia tenderly, takes a single tendril of her hair in his hand and caresses it as though it were a skein of pure gold. 'I love you.'

'I love you, too, Matt. I don't know how it's happened, and happened so fast, but I'm crazy about you.'

'I'm crazy about you. Insane. Insanely in love.'

Julia smiles. 'Maybe we are insane.'

'I don't care.'

❧❧❧

Matt slides away from Julia and rummages on the floor amongst their discarded clothes for the carrier bag he's brought with him. He produces a still-chilled bottle of Bollinger champagne and two champagne flutes. He stands up and Julia can see that his penis is still stiff, sticking out from his body at an upright angle. He unwraps the foil then uncorks the bottle, twisting it around in his palms so that the cork doesn't fly across the room. It gently pops open. Matt pours them both a glass and hands one to Julia, before sitting down on the edge of the bed.

'Cheers. To the most beautiful woman I've ever seen, the sexiest woman I've ever fucked.'

Julia takes her glass, laughs, and chinks his glass.

'To an Adonis who's just totally blown my mind and body.'

They both take a large draft of champagne and Julia glances down from Matt's eyes to his penis, which is still swollen, jutting out from his body. He notices her looking at him and smiles, places his glass on the table by the side of the bed, sits back against the head-board and slides his hand down his body towards his erection. He slowly strokes the length of it with the fingers of his right hand, running one finger over the head which is still glistening from fucking Julia. All the while he looks Julia in the eye and smiles.

Julia moves up the bed, leans over and takes his penis into her mouth, gently pushing it in and caressing the swollen head with her lips, sucking and licking gently. Matt moves his hand aside to allow her access and sighs, heavily, and she continues to suck him for a little while before pulling away and moving up to sit next to him, stretching her legs out languorously and sinking into the sheer joy of being with him.

'You taste lovely' whispers Julia. 'But I want you to masturbate. I'll taste you more, later.'

'Your mouth is amazing' says Matt, reaching out the hand nearest to her and rubbing it over her breasts, cupping each in turn, feeling its weight, gently running his fingers over her nipples which are stiff with excitement. 'And so are your breasts. You're amazing. All of you...'

Matt moves his hand back onto his penis and caresses it gently, sliding his hand up and down the shaft, delicately teasing the swollen head with his fingers, running them around the rim and massaging his foreskin over the shiny, plum-like head.

Julia places her hand between her legs and gently rubs the skin around her clitoris, parting her legs as she does so and sighing deeply.

'Yes, make yourself come, Gigi' murmurs Matt.

He squeezes his penis hard now and starts pumping it with long, regular, strokes of his hand, back and forth. The head is slick, oily and bright scarlet.

His lips part slightly and he breathes heavily, his blue eyes partly closing in euphoria and arousal. Julia cannot believe how beautiful he looks, his firm, muscled body exuding a heavy scent of sex as he masturbates in front of her.

'Kneel up, Matt, in front of me, I want you to come in my mouth' whispers Julia.

Matt swings one leg over Julia's body and kneels in front of her, pumping his stiff penis in front of her lips which she parts, gently licking the head of his cock with long, slow, movements of her soft tongue.

Matt continues pumping the swollen shaft of his penis back and forth, trying to hold back his orgasm. Julia's mouth opens wide and she gasps then moans, her body arching underneath him in ecstasy. On seeing the movement of Julia's breasts beneath him, gently shaking with her orgasm, he can hold onto his own no longer and, bracing himself with one arm against the wall, shoots out several thick streams of spunk which he directs towards Julia's mouth. The white pearlescent liquid catches the top of her hair, then her eyebrows, then her chin before finally shooting over her parted lips. Julia instinctively licks the spunk as it covers her mouth and groans with pleasure before sinking back down onto the bed. Matt moves quickly down the bed and lays on top of her, holding her close, before kissing her deeply on the mouth. After what feels like an eternity of kissing, in which Julia is lost to the feel of his tongue and lips, he pulls away and whispers,

'Everything feels so natural with you, Gigi. I love you.'

'I love you too...' says Julia, quietly, looking into his eyes and gently kissing his neck, against which tendrils of his soft, blond, curly hair rest amidst a sheen of sweat.

Julia sinks into a sleepy reverie. Matt slides off her and lies next to her, lovingly wrapping his arms around her and burying his face in her hair, before drifting off to sleep himself, whilst outside, far below, the traffic roars in the distance and on a nearby roof, the magpie chatters in the evening sunshine.

18

A LITTLE BIT OF SPICE

fter several weeks and three consecutive late evenings working on the Jaffa account with Sandi, Alex is ready to rip her clothes off and bang her right there on the desk. He doesn't know how long he can resist her. She's been giving him sighs and longing looks day in, day out, he knows she wants it.

Figuring it out logically, Julia is asleep when he gets home and leaves for work six hours later. Suddenly they're living separate lives. What is the fucking point of pretending that his crazy relationship with his ex-mother-in-law is actually working? Sandi is perfect, she's got a perfect body, perfect skin, perfect lips, perfect breasts, she's put together like a dream woman. And she wants him.

He sits, hunched over his keyboard, frowning, and runs both hands through his hair. He's jaded, he's exhausted, he's horny and he's out of ideas…any idea that doesn't involve removing all of Sandi's clothes and fucking her for hours on end, that is. He looks at his watch. Six o'clock. Julia will be somewhere in the West End nearby meeting her author friend, Livia. She's staying the night in town. He doesn't have to go back to Tewin.

Sandi slides onto the stool next to him in the hot-desking area and smiles.

' God, every time I look at the screen it's just going round and round in circles. I'm knackered. I guess we'd better get on with it though. One more late night and we've cracked it. Be a shame to stop now.'

'No. Fuck it. Let's go for something to eat.'

'Really? Won't your *girlfriend* mind?'

'It's just something to eat, Sandi. She's off out with a bunch of writers, anyway, they'll be getting out of it somewhere. Girls' night out. You've never seen anything like it, the way a bunch of writers knock it back. She's staying the night in London with them...'

'Oh, I see. She is, is she...'

Alex glances across at Sandi and she's pulled her lips in and is looking at him evenly, with wide, open blue eyes.

'How very *fun* for them.'

'Yeah. So...how about Momo's?'

'The Moroccan place off Regent Street? Never been but heard it's amazing.'

'They've got a terrace, we can sit outside. It's on me.'

'Alex, really, that's just such a lovely idea, thank you.'

❧❧❧

7pm. The magpie's in the City, Alex's girlfriend stretched out on the white sheets of a hotel bed and his ex-wife Kate dozing on her lover's breasts. All Alex cares about is fucking Sandi.

Momo's luscious, Moroccan exterior with its huge pots of palms, bamboo and ivy framing the entrance welcomes them as they walk in from the still sweltering street. A short, Moroccan-looking waiter appears from the depths of the interior balancing several plates of delicious looking, steaming food on one arm. After depositing the plates at a nearby table, he approaches Alex and Sandi.

'Table for two, sir?'

'Yes...please...'

'That one in the corner?' asks Sandi.

The waiter ushers them to a table framed by potted palms and bamboo, slightly apart from the others and produces two menus with a flourish.

'This is nice, Alex. What a great idea. So nice to get away from work.' says Sandi, smiling gently.

'Are you ready to order now? Would you like time to study the menu? Or would you like to order something to drink?' asks the waiter in a flat, professional tone.

'Not ready to order, no, this is our first time. I'll order wine now though.' Alex flicks through the wines on the menu and announces 'A bottle of 2000 Pommery Grand Cru please.'

'The champagne. Yes, sir.' says the waiter, bowing slightly and disappearing into the restaurant's interior.

Sandi smiles and her eyes widen.

'Bloody hell, Alex…'

'It's a special occasion.' says Alex, looking up at Sandi and raising his eyebrows. He picks up his menu and scans through it, a look of displeasure suddenly clouding his face.

'Can't remember the last time I went out for a meal with Julia…'

'Why not?'

'She cooks.'

'Is she any good?'

'Very. That's the problem. We never go out.'

'That must be…boring.'says Sandi, choosing her words carefully.

'Stuck in fucking Tewin. It is.'

The pair peruse their menus in silence and the air feels heavy with unsaid conversation.

The waiter returns with an ice bucket, bottle of champagne and two glasses which he deposits on the table in front of them, artfully squeezing open the champagne cork and pouring a sample of champagne for Alex to try.

'She can try it first.' says Alex and the waiter defers to Sandi by pouring her a drop of champagne.

'Beautiful. Thank you.' says Sandi, before the waiter tops up their glasses and retreats again.

'I...I don't mean to be funny, Alex, but maybe shacking up with your mother-in-law wasn't such a great idea...'

'You *don't say*.' Alex looks up at Sandi who is looking at him innocently, her eyes wide and blue. She smiles, sweetly and her lips look eminently kissable.How can he look at lips like that without wanting to kiss them? 'I want to fuck her.' is suddenly the only thought running through his head.

'What are you going to have, then?' asks Sandi. 'You look ravenous.'

Alex leans back and glances at Sandi across the table.

'I am ravenous. I'm *fucking* ravenous, Sandi.'

'I think I'll have the spinach fataya. Followed by the lamb tagine. What about you?' replies Sandi, ignoring the tone of Alex's voice.

Alex glances down at his menu again. ' The chicken briouats and the Momo grill.' He reads from the menu...'Roast honey quail, lamb cutlet, merguez...no idea what merguez is...'

'A type of Moroccan sausage.' says Sandi, archly.

'Sounds good to me...'

Alex and Sandi both drain their glasses of champagne and the waiter takes their order. They finish the bottle before the starters and Alex orders another bottle, this time wine, the majority of which Alex polishes off during the main course. They finish a third bottle during dessert and by the time they pay the bill, Alex is arse-holed and Sandi is well on the way. It's still only 9pm.

'I don't even want to know what the bill is. You must like me a lot, spending this amount of money on dinner for me, Alex.' says Sandi, coquettishly.

'I do like you. Can't you tell?' Alex looks deep into Sandi's eyes, his focus blurring slightly. It's a long time since he's drunk this much in such short a space of time. 'This has been going on for weeks, Sandi.'

'What?' Sandi's eyes are wide and innocent.

'Us. You and me. This…'

'This what, Alex?' coos Sandi.

'You know what.'

'I know I know what but I want you to tell me what.'

'You, being so beautiful. So irr'sist-urbull.'

'You're so smooth, Alex Harcourt.

'I fucking mean it. You're just…a vision of beauty, swimming before my eyes…'

'So you're really not getting any at home then…'

'I don' wanna fuck Julia'

'So who *do* you want to fuck, Alex?'

The waiter returns with the receipt from their bill and smiles a false, winning smile at Alex.

'I hope you've enjoyed your meal, Sir. And the lady.'

'Fucking awesome.' says Alex.

The waiter grins and retreats, glancing at the little bronze tray on which the receipt lies.

'What were we talking about?'

'We were talking about who you want to fuck…' says Sandi, slightly impatiently.

'Oh yeah. You. That's who I want to fuck. Right now.'

'Here?'

'No not here. There's people everywhere. Let's go back to yours.'

'Are you sure about this, Alex? We've both had quite a lot to drink…I don't want you to regret it tomorrow.'

'I won't fucking regret it. I've wanted you ever since I first set eyes on you. Had to have you. Gorgeous.'

'It's just…you don't sound very like you at the moment…'

'I'm more me than I've been for fucking ages, Sandi. You've made me *me* again.'

'Come on, we'd better go. You're an angel.' smiles Sandi.

They leave the restaurant without leaving a tip.

⁂

Sandi and Alex hail a cab south of the river to Balham. In the cab Alex wraps his arms around Sandi and kisses her, deeply. She folds into him, the kiss feels wet and loose, his lips rubbery. Sandi knows that this is because he's so pissed, but doesn't care. She's got him. In a cab. Headed for her flat. South. Away from Julia.

After getting out of the cab, Alex sways up the path to Sandi's front door and she holds his arm to steady him. Once inside, she flicks the light on inside the hall of her ground-floor flat then leads Alex towards the lounge.

'Just wait here a sec.' says Sandi, leaving Alex in the doorway. She walks into the lounge which is modern Ikea and minimalist. With a thick, white rug. Sandi throws her bag onto the sofa, bends down and rolls the rug up.

'What the fuck are ya doing, Sandi?'

'So it doesn't get dirty.' she mutters, glancing at him.

'I'm not gonna get anything dirty. The only thing I want to get dirty is *you*.'

Sandi sighs deeply, and leads Alex through the lounge towards another door which opens onto the bedroom. Again it's sparse, clean and minimalist. A king-sized bed, a large umbrella plant and vertical blinds.

Alex throws himself onto his back on the bed, his arms and legs spread-eagled. 'Home!' he announces, triumphantly.

Sandi looks at him and starts undressing, slipping off first her dress, then reaching behind her back to unfasten her white, lacy bra to reveal the two perfect orbs of her breasts, the pink nipples hard and pointing upwards, then peeling off her thong, revealing a neatly-trimmed Brazilian.

Alex stares at her, a look of slack lust plastered on his goofy face.

'Cor.'

Sandi moves over to the bed and unbuckles Alex's sandals, removing them, then unfastens his cargo pants and pulls them off too. Then she sits astride Alex and pulls his t-shirt over his head revealing his sun-tanned chest.

'All that rock-climbing, eh? You've got a fantastic tan...' she murmurs.

'All...that...gritstone...' Alex murmurs back to her. 'My lovely mistress. The grit.'

'What are you on about?' laughs Sandi.

Alex ignores her, reaches up and cups Sandi's breasts in his hands.

'Fucking gorgeous tits, Sandi.'

Thanks. Sandi looks at Alex mischievously and peels off his underpants (which are covered with pictures of beefburgers.)

Alex's cock is stiff and springs out once Sandi releases it from its beefburger-patterned prison.

'God, Alex. Beautiful.'

Alex grins proudly, wrapping his arms around Sandi's hips and pulling her towards him. He flips her from her position astride him, turns her over onto her back and rubs his hands all over her body before sliding on top of her, kissing her passionately and guiding his stiff cock into her. She clasps her hands around his bottom and gasps.

'Oh, god, Alex...'

Alex starts fucking Sandi with long strokes and she writhes around underneath him, coming almost immediately, moaning loudly and calling his name over and over. Alex, grunting and thrusting with perspiration dripping from his brow, keeps pummelling into Sandi, back and forth, grinding into her. Gradually his pace begins to slow, his rhythm changes, he pumps once then stops, then starts again, then suddenly slows down to a complete halt and slumps on top of her.

'What's the matter?' asks Sandi. Alex is silent. She tilts his head sideways slightly and looks at his face. His eyes are closed. A drop of saliva drools from his bottom lip and then his lips shudder in a loud snore. Sandi can feel his now limp penis sliding out of her. She pushes Alex off her body and rolls him onto the bed next to her, onto his back, where his mouth drops open and he continues to snore, loudly.

She looks at his body, lying there. Despite his snoring, he's still gorgeous. She loves his body, his flat, hairless, chest glistening in the moonlight slanting through the slats of the blinds.

Although she's had a vaginal orgasm, Sandi still feels unbearably horny. She slides one leg over Alex's prone leg and shakes his shoulder.

'Alex...wake up...'

His head jerks a little in response and he stutters another loud snore.

Sandi squeezes Alex's leg between her own legs as she watches him. He's absolutely beautiful. His curly hair, his gorgeous face. She can't believe that he's here in bed with her at last, after desiring him for so long. She unconsciously starts grinding her pussy against him as she strokes his chest, runs her hands over his face and through his hair. She's feeling unbearably horny and finds herself thrusting her hips back and forth, her pussy slick and oily now, sliding over Alex's skin. His leg feels huge between her thighs, she can hardly contain her excitement, as she rubs herself against him she imagines his leg is a huge penis on which she's riding. She keeps grinding and sliding, her breasts jiggling up and down with her movements. She starts breathing heavily and moaning out loud. She holds onto Alex's chest as she rides his leg, moving her hips to and fro faster and faster, shaking her head from side to side, her blonde hair falling over her face, her lips parted, her eyes half-closed. Her pussy is aching unbearably now as she grinds into him and she feels her orgasm rushing up from inside her and overwhelming her. She cries out as she comes, rhythmically thrusting against Alex's leg, sliding back and forth until eventually she subsides onto him, spreading her arms over him and sinking onto his leg in delighted reverie before drifting softly to sleep, content in the knowledge that wherever Julia is, getting drunk with her no-doubt snobby literary friends, she's not with Alex, for she, Sandi has him now.

19

WHISPERINGS

nother magpie sits on the windowsill outside Christina's bedroom window, cackling and chattering loudly. Maybe it's the same one. Christina wouldn't know, the morning has brought with it exhaustion after hours making love with Kate the previous evening. Christina understands that Kate had to return home ready for an early morning hair appointment, but wishes she'd cancelled. Her hurried departure of the night before has left a bed with just Christina in it, which suddenly, for the first time in as long as she can remember, feels empty. There's something about Kate...

Matt and Julia are wrapped around one another in bed, immune to the first light of dawn, having made love seven times and then curling up in blissful contentment around 2am.

'There's nothing to feel guilty about now Alex is sniffing round this Sandi woman...' Julia keeps telling herself. Matt has put Kate out of his mind. He'll deal with her when he has to. It's over.

※ ※ ※

Alex sleeps through the gentle haze of dawn and on into the full morning sun glaring through the blinds which Sandi has flicked opened wide. He groggily opens his eyes and sees her in silhouette against the blinds as he squints, her figure perfectly languid in a thin, floaty, transparent shirt through which he can see her breasts, the nipples pointing at him.

'Fuck. My head. What happened?'

'You've forgotten already?' Sandi grins and sashays over to him bearing a pint glass of water, puts it down on the little table beside the bed, leans over and kisses him on the mouth, her breasts wobbling slightly as she bends over.

'I'm here. At yours. Fuck. How did we get home?'

'My home, Alex, not yours. We caught a cab. You were completely arseholed. You drank most of the last two bottles of wine.'

'Oh...'

'But it was mint.' Sandi smiles, radiantly, lies down next to Alex and starts stroking his body all over.

'Sandi, I've got to go. What time is it?'

'Ten.'

'Shit. Julia doesn't deserve this. She's done nothing wrong. Fuck. What have I done?'

Sandi stops stroking him and sits up, abruptly.

'Er....excuse me...National Portrait Gallery? Snogging some other bloke?'

'I don't believe that for a minute. You saw the state Kate was in. She's made the whole thing up just to cause trouble. She hates Julia for being with me, she'd do anything to split us up.'

'I know she would, but what kind of person would actually invent a crazy story like that?'

'A *Kate* type of person. You don't know her, Sandi, she's fucking *nuts*.'

'OK but what if she is telling the truth? If Julia's having an affair, she fucking well deserves this and you deserve better than her. You deserve someone who understands you. Who understands the way your *mind* operates, who understands your *work*, who understands your *body*...'

'Yeah...' says Alex, distractedly, his head pounding, his mouth dry. He jumps off the bed and starts to grab his clothes, hurriedly getting dressed.

'You got any Ibuprofen?'

'Hold on...' Sandi goes to fetch some pain relief then returns, handing the tablets to Alex and offering him the glass of water he hasn't touched.

'Do you fancy breakfast? There's a great place round the corner...'

'Nah...no Sandi, I'd better get back. I feel awful.'

Sandi leaves Alex to get dressed, grabs some clothes of her own and goes into the bathroom to dress privately. The twat. So this is his game is it? Fuck and dump. When she emerges from the bathroom, Alex is dressed and standing by the lounge window, running his hands through his dishevelled hair and looking out at the street, where a man is arguing with a woman over a parking space.

'So...you're going?' asks Sandi, crisply.

'Yeah. Look, thanks for letting me crash here. We'll pick up on the Jaffa account on Monday, yeah?'

'Fine.' says Sandi, and leads him to the front door feeling utterly crushed. He pecks her on the cheek goodbye. He couldn't say it more clearly if he tried. She's been a one-night stand.

She returns to the bedroom and glumly stares at the rumpled sheet and duvet. She pulls the duvet cover, pillow cases and sheet from the bed, marches to the kitchen and stuffs them in the washing machine, putting them on a hot wash. Fucking Alex. She should have known. She needs to talk to someone. Christina.

❧❧❧

Sandi: Hi darling, long time no see. Thought I'd just give you a bell to catch up. I'm not disturbing you, am I?

Christina: No it's OK. I'm just doing the very glamorous job of cleaning bird shit off the bedroom windowsill. What are you up to?

Sandi: God, where do I start?

Christina: Oooh, what's happened? Good or bad?

Sandi: Both.

Christina: Go on…

Sandi: There's someone at work…I've mentioned him before, Alex…

Christina: Oh yeah you did, that gorgeous guy with curly hair, right?

Sandi: That's him. Well…it finally happened.

Christina: You shagged him?

Sandi: Yup.

Christina: What was it like?

Sandi: Awesome. We went to Momo's last night then went back to mine. He's gorgeous. The only thing is, you know, he's living with this woman Julia, she's really old, fifty-six or something, ancient. She's a writer or something…

Christina: Right…

Sandi: And this morning he rushed off back to her. Even though I strongly suspect the stupid cow's shagging someone else.

Christina: How come?

Sandi: Her daughter - who happens to be his ex-wife, don't even get me started on that one - she stormed into the agency last week screeching about how she'd just seen her mother wrapped around some bloke at The National Portrait Gallery.

Christina: The National Portrait Gallery? What's his surname?

Sandi: Harcourt. Alex Harcourt…why?

Christina: Oh…nothing…I…I just wondered, thought I might have met him through work.

Sandi: I thought you were mainly doing fashion now?

Christina: Yeah I am...anyway...so...well...what a bastard, rushing off. Poor you...

Sandi (suddenly bursting into tears): I'm sorry, Christina...I didn't mean to offload on you...he's...he's been after me for weeks...I think I've done something really stupid...he's obviously still in love with this woman he lives with, he couldn't wait to get away...I mean, after a first night with someone you really get on with...it's not just physical...we've been working together on this project for so long...we're like soul mates...and to have this amazing night with them and they just run off...I feel totally humiliated...

Christina: Darling. See what happens. He's probably completely freaked out...you know what some blokes are like after the first night, they think you're going to tie them to your bed and keep them there...

Sandi: No...it's not him. It's *her*. She's obviously still got this *massive* hold over him. *Bitch.*

Christina: Well they *are* living together...

Sandi (glumly): I know. Fuck. What a mess.

ᘏᘏᘏ

Christina: Kate? Are you home?

Kate: Yeah...tired...

Christina: Me too...

Kate: Yeah...

Christina: That was lovely...last night...

Kate: I know...it was...I want to...let's...

Christina: Yes, let's...soon...

Kate: Yeah...soon...

Christina: So, is Matt there?

Kate: Nope. He's been out all night. *Wanker*. I know exactly where he'll be. With my *mother* somewhere. If you read this in a book you'd never believe it, it's just too surreal.

Christina: Well, something else surreal has just happened…I just got a phone call from an old friend of mine, Sandi…

Kate: *Sandi?*

Christina: She works at Bates & Bartle…

Kate: That's the company *Alex* works for…don't tell me…she's not the one who's got something going on with Alex, is she?

Christina: Well, I didn't know that before, but I do now.

Kate: So she's called *Sandi*, is she? And she's your *friend?*

Christina: *Old* friend. We don't *chill* together any more. She's quite *straight*.

Kate: I can't believe what I'm hearing here…

Christina: Look Kate, let me make this clear. After last night… my loyalties are with you, OK? Which is why I'm calling you…

Kate: OK…thanks…so what did she say?

Christina: She told me all about last night. Your suspicions were bang on. They went out for a meal after work and went back to hers. Where he shagged her.

Kate: Such a predictable fucking *twat*.

Christina: *However* it's not all roses in the castle. She sounded quite upset. Apparently he fucked off home this morning feeling guilty about his girlfriend, who, I guess, is your mum, right? Julia? The writer?

Kate: Yup. That's her. Batshit crazy hormonal nightmare.

Christina: To be honest, Kate, he sounds like a complete tosser.

Kate: He is.

Christina: I mean, he shags your mum behind your back, moves in with her to your *family home*, gets bored or whatever, then shags his colleague and *craps* on her. The world is fucking *heaving* with tossers like him. They think they can walk on any woman they like.

Kate: I know. Cunts. The lot of them. Women don't behave like that.

Christina: I know, sweetheart. Men don't have that compassionate gene that we have.

Kate: It's just in our bones.

Christina: We support one another.

Kate: I know, babes.

Christina: So…what are you going to do about it? Are you going to tell your mum?

Kate: D'you know what? I can't be arsed. I cannot fucking well be bothered with any of them. It's all so *incestuous*. I wish I could just fuck off somewhere abroad and *leave them all to it.* I've already told my mother about Alex and Sandi, *she'll* have to sort it out.

Christina: I'd like to fuck off abroad too, actually. That's exactly what I need after the past few months…

Kate: Fuck it. Let's do it, Christina. Let's just fuck off…

Christina: Well, how does this sound? I've got a mate, Marcus, he lives in a tiny mountain village in Andalusia, it's really picturesque. He's a jazz trumpeter. He tours for most of the year and he's always told me to just come and use his house whenever I want. I even know where his spare keys are hidden outside.

Kate: What's the place called?

Christina: Frigiliana. It wins awards for being the most picturesque village in Spain. White houses scattered over the hillside, views across luscious groves of the sea in the distance…

Kate: Frigiliana…

Christina: I could get some shots for my landscape portfolio…

Kate: I've got some holiday to use up at work, my boss keeps nagging me to take it before the end of the month…

Christina: Shall I start looking at flights?

Kate: *Yes! Let's do it! As* soon as you find a flight message me the details and we'll book. Let's go like, *asap!*

Christina: It's Saturday…how about Monday for a week?

Kate: *Hell* yes! Let's get out of this fucking shit hole, leave these arseholes behind and *fly!*

20

AT THE CAFÉ BOHÈME IN SOHO

N o sooner has Kate clicked off the phone from Christina than it rings again. Colin.

Colin: Babes! Seems like ages since we caught up!

Kate: It was a month ago, Colin, when I left you at Harry Styles' mother's party, remember?

Colin: Seems like a lot longer. Always does when I don't see you.

Kate: You were a prat that night, Colin. You embarrassed me in front of everyone.

Colin: Yeah well, those Yummy Mummies were a right bunch of stuck-up cunts.

Kate: Because none of them thought your jokes were funny?

Colin: Sense of humour disorder. Probably a bunch of lesbos as well.

Kate: You can't say 'lesbos' anymore, Colin. Anyway I thought you loved the idea of lesbians. You've always said you wanted a threesome.

Colin: Yeah, with *gorgeous women*. Not with the woolly hat and dungarees brigade.

Kate: They were hardly that, Colin, they were sophisticated women…

Colin: …up their own arses. Anyway, babes, fancy meeting up for a drink?

Kate: Actually, Colin, I do. A lot's happened...I could do with someone to talk to...who understands...I'm going away on Monday for a week...

Colin: Where to?

Kate: Spain.

Colin: Who with? Not that dickhead boyfriend of yours?

Kate: No, not Matt...a new...friend of mine...Christina... she's a fashion photographer...

Colin: Fit?

Kate: Very. She looks like Penelope Cruz. But she's....taken, actually...I think...

Colin: Bet her boyfriend's a tosser.

Kate: Well...yeah...anyway...I could meet you this afternoon?

Colin: Café Bohème on Old Compton Street?

Kate: The one on the corner, opposite the theatre? With the benches outside?

Colin: Bingo, babes. 3pm?

Kate: It's a date.

Sunday. 3pm. Café Bohème. Old Compton Street.

For the first time in days, the heat has dropped and it's cloudy. Kate's glad, she's been fed up with sweat-stained clothes and smearing foundation. She's wearing black cotton capri pants, flat red pumps and a peppermint green cotton shirt, tied at the waist with the top buttons undone, revealing her delicate cleavage and pink lacy bra. She sits on an empty bench and orders a bottle of wine. Colin, predictably, is late. She sits watching pedestrians walk past alone or in groups, talking, until suddenly Colin's there in front of her.

Colin: Daydreaming as usual...you look hot...a table...great!

Kate: Hi, Colin.

At the Café Bohème in Soho

Colin sits down, removes his jacket, stretches his arms wide and yawns.

Colin: Hot, innit?

Kate: It's better...

Colin: So...what's been happening in Kate world then?

Kate: I don't know where to start, Colin. You wouldn't believe it.

Colin: The Northerner's turned out to be gay. Always knew it.

Kate: No...but I'm pretty sure he's shagging my mother.

Colin: *What?* I thought your mother was shacked up with your ex, that other wanker, Alex.

Kate: She is. But, unbelievably, she met Matt after a bomb scare at the National Portrait Gallery and they've started seeing each other. I caught them the other day, I found out where he was going and just turned up and saw them, kissing in broad daylight, in front of everyone. It was disgusting.

Colin: *Fuck!*

Kate: But get this. Matt was calling her *'Gigi'*! She was pretending to be someone else! She's totally fucking lost it, I tell you Colin.

Colin: Why would she do that?

Kate: I suppose it's because of her stupid *books*. Because she's going *incognito* or something. She's such a fucking *drama queen.*

Colin: So...let me get this straight...Northern twat is shagging your mother...

Kate: I don't know that it's gone that far yet...they were kissing...

Colin: OK then, *about to* shag your mother...but *he doesn't know she's your mother?*

Kate: Correct...

Colin: So, did you tell him? What did you do?

Kate: I wanted to kill them both but I felt sick. I just had to get out of there. She's a fucking liability. A maniac. Her old-person's hormones have gone into overdrive or something, she needs fucking locking up.

Colin: Incredible, babes. Your life's like a fucking movie!

Kate: So I went to Alex's agency. To snitch on her. And guess what I walked into *there*?

Colin: Alex with his cock in some bloke's mouth?

Kate: No, Colin. But what I did see was Alex all over this trollop he works with.

Colin: I know a few people at B&B...what's she look like?

Kate: Tall, blonde, trashy...

Colin: Drop dead gorgeous with fantastic tits? Blue eyes?

Kate: *Fake* tits.

Colin whips out his iPhone and looks at the B&B Creative Team page, finds a photograph of Sandi and shows Kate.

Colin: Is this her?

Kate: Yes.

Colin: *Fuck! Sandi! I know her!* She's secretly got this thing about me. Bumped into her at the Loophole opening a couple of months back.

Kate: Really?

Colin: Yeah. She's full of herself but I'd do her...so...what do you mean by 'all over each other'? How 'all over'?

Kate: Alex had his hand on her arse.

Colin: Yeah, she likes that. So, do you think they're fucking each other then?

Kate: I wasn't sure...but my friend, Christina, the one I'm going to Spain with, is an old friend of Sandi's. And this morning, Sandi rings Christina up and tells her she spent last night with Alex. So yeah, they're fucking one another.

Colin: Jesus…so…Sandi's fucking your mother's boyfriend? I bet she'd like to know about *that!*

Kate: Well I'm not telling her. That's one reason I'm going to Spain, I just want to get away from the lot of them.

Colin: You do right, Kate, stay out of it. I would…

Kate: There's something else…

Colin: Go on, surprise me.

Kate: Christina, the photographer…she's not just a friend… we're actually…lovers…

Colin (spluttering his wine): *What?* Let me see a photo of her!

Kate googles Christina's website and shows Colin a picture of Christina wearing black leather trousers, white vest, legs apart and carrying a huge camera, her head down and looking through the lens at a baby panda eating a stalk of bamboo.

Colin: Fucking hell, Kate! She's unbelievable!

Kate: Yeah…she's gorgeous.

Colin: How come you never told me you were a rug-muncher?

Kate: A what?

Colin: A lezza.

Kate: Colin, I've told you. You can't use derogatory language like that anymore.

Colin: So why didn't you tell me you do threesomes?

Kate: Because I don't. I didn't say we had a threesome. We made love. Together. Without anyone else there.

Colin: Oh fucking hell, Kate, how can you do this to me? Shut up already! You have got to let me in on this one babes!

Kate: Let you *in* on it?

Colin: Yeah! You've got to let me have a piece of this action, babes, she's a fucking stunner!

Kate: What on earth are you talking about, Colin?

Colin: You, me and Penelope fucking Cruz, that's what! You know you want to. Look. I'll bring a few bottles of Cristal and a gram of coke and we party, yeah?

Kate: You have got to be out of your mind, Colin.

Colin: Nah babes, nah. Not out of my mind. This is just the most brilliant opportunity ever. I could fucking film it! We could sell it and make a shit-load!

Kate: I think I'm in love with her. I've got no intention of doing anything so ridiculously seedy, Colin, don't be such a fucking *dick*.

Colin takes a long slug of his white wine and leans back, a self-satisfied smile on his stupid, arrogant face.

Colin: Just you wait, babes. A week or two of fanny fur and you'll both be gagging for a pork sword.

Kate: You're disgusting. But I love you all the same.

Colin: So I'm forgiven for Harry Styles then?

Kate: Forgiven.

Colin: Fucking hell, a mouthful of pussy and you're tame as a lamb. Wish I'd known that when I was going out with you.

Kate: I feel wonderful…listen…I have a favour to ask, actually…

Colin: What?

Kate: I don't want to go back to Hemel Hempstead. I don't even want to talk to Matt. I've packed for Spain, I was wondering if I could crash on your sofa for a couple of nights till Christina and I leave? I know she's got some work on and I don't want to impose on her…

Colin: Course, babes! And meantime, I'll keep trying to persuade you to bring Señorita Cruz back round for a party!

21

LOVE AMONGST THE TURRETS

y the time Julia arrives home it's midday. She walks up the drive towards her front door as though sailing on air. She feels dizzy through lack of sleep and heady with love.

Alex is in the kitchen, standing over the juicer shoving apples and pears into the shaft as the motor roars. He notices Julia, flicks the switch off and slowly, the juicer's blade stops rotating and it comes to a halt. Julia stares at it and then looks up at Alex. He looks worried, furtive and uneasy as he glances at her and then removes the jug of juice, walks across the kitchen and pours the juice into a pint glass.

'You look a bit rough, Alex.'

'Yeah. I stayed up late. Drinking whisky. Probably had too much. What about you? How did it go with Livia?'

'Fantastic. We had a brilliant time.'

'Where'd you go?'

'The French House. Stayed there all night.'

'Fuckin' hell, Julia, The fucking *French House?* It's so pretentious.'

'No, it isn't. And we ran into Colin Firth. Livia knows him.'

'Colin *Firth?* Since when were you a *Colin Firth* fan?'

'I'm not, particularly, although I loved him in *Dutch Girls.*'

Alex takes a swig of his apple and pear juice and glares at Julia through his guilt-ridden, head-banging hangover which won't disappear despite Sandi's Ibuprofen.

'Never heard of it.'
'Before your time. You'd have been a baby when that was on T.V.'
'Right. Look I'm going back to bed. I feel shit.'
'You look like you've been up all night.'
'Well I haven't. I need sleep though.'

Alex stomps off upstairs leaving Julia alone in the kitchen looking at the juicer which Alex hasn't even bothered to rinse out. It suddenly occurs to her that she hates him. Just like that. He suddenly seems like an interloper in her house.

Julia goes into the garden out of hearing of the upstairs bedroom and rings Matt.

Julia: Hi Matt.
Matt: Hi Gigi.
Julia: I just got home.
Matt: Me too.
Julia: Alex is here. He's just gone to bed with a hangover. Says he was here last night and drunk loads of whisky but he's lying. Look, I don't care, anyway. It's over with him. I just want him to go. What about you?
Matt: Kate isn't here. She's left a note. I presume this means I'm dumped.
Julia: What does it say?
Matt: That she's gone to stay with her ex, Colin, and then she's going to Spain for a week with some girlfriend she's only just met. Well that's a load of crap. She'll be going with Colin.

So they're back together. He really is a prize tosser. Good luck to them. Fuck 'em.

Julia: What are you doing for the rest of the weekend? I don't think I can wait until next week to see you…

Matt: Working on Sunday but you could come round here until then if you want, I mean Kate's not here…

Julia: No…no it's OK…she wouldn't like that…it wouldn't be right.

Matt: Nor is us spending all night fucking one another, Gigi, but we did it.

Julia: Not in her home we didn't. I couldn't.

Matt: It's quite touching that you're so concerned for her. You shouldn't be. She's a spoilt brat.

Julia: Yes…it seems…

Matt: Why don't you come along on Sunday then? We're shooting a Vuitton ad at Knebworth House, it's right round the corner from Tewin.

Julia: That sounds perfect. I could do with having a bath and an early night after last night, I'm exhausted. Worth it though…

Matt: It was…so…do you want to come and meet me? They won't let you on set unfortunately because of this brand privacy thing but I can see you straight after.

Julia: Sure, what time?

Matt: If you turn up at 11am when they open to the public, we'll be almost finished by then, just ring me when you get to the main entrance. We did a day here last week, they're really helpful. We can go for lunch somewhere afterwards.

Julia: Sounds perfect. I'll see you tomorrow.

Julia's mind is going round in circles. She can't believe that once again she's fallen in love with her daughter's partner, a partner her daughter neither appreciates nor loves, a partner who is too good for her daughter. But her maternal instincts are driving her crazy, she feels like a traitor and at some level hates what she's doing. She collapses into a hot, scented bath and washes Matt's sweat and juices from her skin, sinking deep into the foamy water and trying to switch off her mind. What will be, will be. Life is stranger than fiction and she's starting to get used to these crazy situations.

❧❧❧

Thankfully, Sunday brings yet another day of glorious sunshine; this has been the nicest August for as long as Julia can remember and a perfect opportunity to take her recently acquired Alfa Romeo Giulia Spider for a spin. She was sorry to sell the old V Dub but had always dreamed of owning a Giulia and she figured life is short so just buy one, she can afford it, after all. Alex said she shouldn't get a classic car but something modern. She ignored him.

Knebworth House is only a few miles away, the drive, with the roof down and the gorgeous tactile feel of the Spider, the engine throbbing in all its vintage ecstasy, calm Julia down and yet energise her at the same time.

Turning off the A1M at the entrance, a surge of electricity shoots through Julia's body. Suddenly she feels unbearably aroused. Meeting Matt after his shoot. Lunch. No time for sex then. 'I have to fuck him though.' is all that's running through her mind and body which have become fused with a driving desire for him.

Just up the driveway Julia pulls over and rings Matt.

Julia: I'm here, down by the ticket office.
Matt: Hi Gigi. Tell them you're with the Vuitton shoot and ask for directions to the car park and the shoot and they'll let you through. See you in ten.

Love Amongst the Turrets

Julia: OK…

Cruising along the long tree-lined avenue leading up the house itself, the breeze in her hair, the sun dappling down through the trees and casting her bare shoulders in warmth, Julia realises she's not felt a happiness like this for a long time, even before she met Alex. Maybe Alex was the catalyst to getting over her husband dying, and Matt is now the real thing, who knows? Is it so ridiculous to meet a man and just know that he's special, that he's different, that he takes your breath away, that even though he might not be right for you, right now it feels like he *is* you? He's inside and outside and everything you see is filtered through his eyes, you can smell him, feel him and long to have him wrap his arms around you and bury his face in your hair. He's all around you and filling your mind with swimming, shifting visions of him which make you feel unsteady on your feet and question whether the world has suddenly shifted on its axis to make you feel so unbalanced…Julia doesn't care whether this is normal or what this means, all that she knows is that she wants Matt and has to be near him.

Standing in the gardens behind the main house, the photographer's assistant is looking at a page of notes on his iPad, his head bent down towards Matt, deep in discussion with him.

Assistant: OK, we've covered everything for today. That's gonna be it for now, mate. We'll see you tomorrow, yeah?

Matt: It's been great. Cheers for your help, see you tomorrow, yeah.

A marquee has been set up to cater for all the personnel on the three day shoot. Matt heads for the wardrobe area and gets changed into his standard jeans and white t-shirt before sitting down at the make-up station and removing his make-up. His mobile rings. It's Gigi, down by the ticket office. Crap, she's waiting for me. He hurriedly pulls on his cowboy boots, looks in the mirror again and tousles his hair a little.

We talked about meals, restaurants. Where are we going to go? Shit I hadn't thought of that. I should've planned this a bit better. He instantly feels guilty, all he's been thinking about since dawn is this Vuitton shoot, mentally preparing for the kind of vibe the creative director and his team had already prepped him about. Bollocks. Maybe Gigi would fancy seeing some of the house they were shooting in this morning, up in the turrets where the public can't go? If anyone questions him, he can say he left something up there. Yeah that'd impress her, standing on top of a fucking turret. She'd feel like a princess then. Plan.

Just as Matt finishes gathering his stuff together to leave, a runner walks into the marquee looking slightly nervous.

Runner: 'You're Matt, right?'
Matt: 'Yeah.'
Runner: 'Someone to see you, buddy. Gigi she says she's called…'
Matt: 'Aye. I'm expecting her. I'll be right out.'

And there she is. Standing in the sunlight, a smile so radiant it lights up her face and puts the sun to shame. She's wearing a floral chiffon dress. Matt glances down at her breasts and then immediately stops himself and looks back at her face. Work is suddenly forgotten. Now he wants her. He walks over to her and wraps his arms around her, holding her close and burying his face in her hair. She draws her breath in, sharply, as she brushes her face against the side of his. Feeling the warmth of his body so close to hers makes her feel faint, she is completely overcome with desire.

Matt: Mmmm. Gigi. You smell divine. It's good to see you again.

Julia: You too…

Matt pulls away and looks at her steadily, a cheeky grin passing over his face.

Matt: Have you ever been here before?

Julia: Not for years…

Matt: Are you hungry? Can you wait a while? There's something I wanted to show you…

Julia: I'm hungry. I want to see what you have to show me, though…

Matt: Come with me. It's amazing, Gigi.

Matt takes Julia's hand and leads her towards a small side entrance of the main house, old Tudor brickwork covered now in Victorian red brick and resplendent in gargoyles, gryphons and Jacobean minarets. A video crew who have been filming a 'making of' documentary about the fashion shoot (*The Making of Victorian Gothic Vuitton*) are packing away silver and black boxes of equipment. The assistant cameraman nods hello at Matt in recognition, who nods back and then leads Julia through a tiny doorway into a dark corridor lined with dark oak-panelled walls and lit with brass wall sconces containing electric candles casting a haunted, flickering light. Matt beckons Julia to follow him and they keep walking further and further deep into the interior of the house.

Suddenly, to the left is a small stone spiral staircase, curling off out of view above them. Matt looks back at Julia and grins again.

Matt: Up here…

Julia: Are we allowed? This part isn't open to the public, right?

Matt: No, we've booked it for the duration of the shoot, don't worry. Access all areas, me, luv.

Matt winks at Julia and she laughs, her pussy already aching with desire. Wherever Matt takes her, she hopes it's private. She wants to fuck him and doesn't think she can sit through lunch in some pub first. This has to be now.

She follows him up the cool, stone spiral staircase which seems to go on forever, until eventually they turn the last corner and the steps open out onto a small room, lined with wood-panelling and several doors, furnished only with an upholstered rocking chair sitting empty in the corner. Next to the single mullioned window letting the sunlight in from outside is a heavier wooden door which Matt pushes open and walks through, his head stooped to avoid the supporting beam.

Julia gasps. The door has opened out onto a small, castellated area on the roof of the stately home, square in shape with a small round turret on each of three corners and a larger turret on the fourth. Julia rushes to the edge and peers over, realising that they are standing atop the largest turret of the house. She looks up and beyond her stretches the gardens, fountains and woods, and there, in the distance, just glimpsed through the sun-drenched trees, the distant dry ribbon of motorway from where she'd arrived less than half an hour ago.

Now, she's suddenly in another world. She turns to look at Matt, her face incredulous with joy.

Julia: Matt, we're on the turret!

Matt: I know. Do you like it my queen?

Julia: My liege, I do. I absolutely fucking love it. It's amazing!

Matt: For now, it is ours.

Julia smiles coquettishly and turns her back to him, leaning her elbows on one castellated prong of the turret wall and sighing, contentedly. Matt walks towards her and wraps his arms around her from behind, pushing his face into her hair and running his hands up and down her body.

Matt: I love your enthusiasm. Your lust for life. Your verve. Your joy. There's not a cynical bone in your body, is there?
Julia: There is when it comes to agents…

Julia looks over her shoulder and laughs as Matt lifts his head up from her hair. She rests her face against his and the warm smell of him overpowers her. She parts her lips and he kisses her, deeply, moving his hands onto her breasts which feel full and soft and warm under the light fabric of her dress. He reaches down the front and slides his hand under her bra, feeling for her nipple which is already stiff and erect. He caresses its tip with his fingers and immediately feels unbearably aroused. He presses against her from behind, she can feel the hard bulge of his penis pressing against her bottom.

Matt pushes his hands under her dress and lifts it right up to her waist, exposing her white, lacy knickers, whilst continuing to kiss her. His mouth feels so soft, Julia feels like she's melting on the spot and can feel her knickers becoming moist and sticky. Matt pushes two fingers under the fabric of her knickers and slides them across the folds of her pussy which are now slippery. Julia gasps and breaks off the kiss, murmuring 'Fuck me. Now.'

Matt unbuttons his jeans, reaches in and flips out his stiff, swollen penis. Julia simultaneously pulls aside the fabric of her knickers. She can feel the swollen head of his penis rubbing against the oily folds of her vulva and raises her bottom slightly to ease his entrance. Matt grabs her hips, pulling her even closer, and pushes his cock into her with one long, deep thrust. Julia cries out loud with the relief of his filling her. He pulls his stiff cock all the way out and then plunges in back into her, Julia flops down against the castellated top of the turret wall, her breasts now squashed against the warm stone and pushes her bottom out even more to facilitate Matt's penis. It feels huge inside her, it feels like too long since they fucked, even though it was only two days before. She realises that she wants this all the time, his cock filling her up, sliding in and out of her. She can smell the sweet smell of his skin and his moans fill her with unbearable desire. Suddenly she feels the whole of her insides shuddering as she orgasms. Matt pulls her up and cups his hands around her breasts, squeezing them through the fabric, then pulls her dress from her shoulders and quickly unclasps her bra before holding the full weight of her breasts in his hands, his fingers trapping each engorged nipple between them. He lowers his face to her neck and sucks and kisses her skin, she smells unbearably good, the feel of her hot, tight pussy as he rams into her again and again is too much and he explodes in a ferocious orgasm, fountaining thick spurts of spunk deep inside her as she groans and whimpers with pleasure. He slows down and rests inside her, breathing into her neck and hair as she raises her head up and slowly turns her face round to his.

Julia: God. Did that just happen?

Matt: I love you, Gigi. There's something…I don't know what it is. You're just so full, and ripe and fucking sexy…you're beautiful.

Julia: So are you. I love you too. I love this, I love everything.

Julia turns back to look into the distance. Standing there in the open air on top of the turret, her breasts and shoulders open to the breeze and sunshine, her face in profile a mask of deep satisfaction and contentment, Matt realises that she's more perfect than anything they've been filming today. She's not fake, like an ad, she's 100% real, flesh and hot-blooded woman.

Julia reaches her arms out wide towards the lush, green countryside beyond the turret of the stately home and murmurs with a sigh, 'The world is mine.'

22

MOJITO AMOR

onday. It's been a shit day. Alex hasn't answered Sandi's texts all weekend and he's taken the day off work. Avoiding her, no doubt. At least there's the saving grace of Julian and Gemma's networking do at Barrio's tonight. Actually, come to think of it, Alex was due to go to that. Sandi wonders whether he'll turn up and feels a frisson of excitement in her groin. Shit. She never planned for this to happen. She's caring too much about what Alex does and doesn't do. This was meant to be enjoyable. It has been enjoyable, the flirting, for weeks now. But sleeping together has changed everything. As it always does. And he was crap in bed. She feels like a fool. Shit, shit shit.

By 6pm Sandi is ready to let her hair down and party. So what if it's Monday night and who gives a flying one about work tomorrow?

Walking up Shoreditch High Street in the late afternoon sun in pink stilettos and a short, floaty dress in mint green chiffon, her blonde hair up in a sloppy bun, tendrils falling down over oversize, black sunglasses, the large glass of white wine she's already drunk fizzing through her body making her feel light and mellow, Sandi suddenly doesn't give a toss about Alex or his stupid girlfriend.

Men glance at her as they walk past her. Women coldly and studiously look the other way in an attempt to beat her in the inevitable and invisible competition that occurs whenever two attractive female strangers walk towards one another on the street. As they approach one another and then pass, the one who looks at the other loses. The one who feigns complete ignorance and indifference to the other wins. Sandi couldn't give a shit. She feels great now, her make-up is perfectly applied, her mobile fully charged, she is armed for social battle.

'East London Creative Cross-Platform Initiative' is taking place in the 'Barrio Boom Boom Room' right at the back of the garishly lit Barrio East, through the jarring, random, crazily-coloured geometric LSD decor, past the bar lit with suspended lampshades in 90s acid-house pink, yellow, turquoise and green and just after the little picture of the swimming man on the wall, pointing to the toilets.

Colin Farmer is already ensconced in the corner of the Boom Boom Room with his free plastic cup of wine and a sulk plastered on his face. This is going to be shit unless some decent women turn up.

Over the next quarter of an hour, smartly dressed, neatly coiffured people drift into the room, each bearing a glass of wine or fruit juice complements of ELCCPI. Beards stopped being hip over eighteen months ago, but most of the men are still sporting them, including a few with their hair scraped up into ghastly, pretentious top knots. The women are all slim, smiling and confident.

'Now this is what I call a cherry-picking room' thinks Colin, as he slouches on the arm of a leather sofa, his slightly too tight pointed leather ankle boots on the nearest table, his arm across the back of the sofa. But none of these women are up to his standard. He can't be arsed to even talk to them. His heart isn't in it.

Until he sees her.

That bird from the Loophole opening a few months back. What was her name? Something beginning with 'S'…

Armed with his luke warm cup of wine, Colin strides confidently over to her, bumping into a bloke with a topknot on the way, who glances down his nose in Colin's direction. Is he worth accidentally spilling some wine over? Probably not, there's a queue for the freebies now to top up again.

Sandi sees him approaching her through the crowd and her heart sinks. That's the complete tool who was bothering her at that do the other month. Fuck. He's heading straight for me.

Colin: Well well well. Look who we have here...looking stunning as usual...I meet so many gorgeous women in my line of work it's hard to remember all their names...Sunny, wasn't it?

Sandi: *Sandi.*

Colin: (pointing both index fingers at her at once, sharp-shooter style) Sun and sand, go together like cheese and pickle. Easy to confuse. So...

Sandi: I was headed over there, actually...

Colin: Sandi...yes...I guess you've forgotten my name. That hurts my feelings...

Sandi: I haven't forgotten. Colin Farmer. How could I forget?

Colin: You flatter me.

Sandi: I'm not trying to flatter you. I'm good with names. And I, too, go to a lot of networking functions. Remembering names is all part of it, wouldn't you agree? Although you forgot mine..

Colin: You care. That's nice to hear. I knew you did...

Sandi: I didn't say I cared. I said I'd remembered your name...

Colin: I could tell you liked me the first time we spoke...

Sandi: Why are you talking to me? I don't like your tone of voice. I didn't like it last time we met and I like it even less, now.

Colin: Well you're still here, aren't you? Why don't you go and talk to one of the many buffoons in the room. There's loads to choose from.

Sandi: I've actually got a partner, thank you very much.

Colin: (staring into her eyes, pointedly) So I heard...

Sandi: What do you mean?

Colin: Oh, so you're not in so much of a rush to go and talk to one of those wankers any more, are you?

Sandi: Are you threatening me?

Colin: Threatening? You're being paranoid, darling. This is meant to be a light-hearted networking event. There's always some hysterical woman has to make it heavy. I don't think the organisers would be very happy if I told them about your snotty attitude, *Sandi*.

Sandi: You haven't answered my question. What do you mean by 'So I heard'?

Colin: It's all over East London.

Sandi: What is?

Colin: You. And that dickhead from B&B, Alex.

Sandi can feel the colour draining from her face. She was on the point of walking away from this complete arsehole...

Sandi: I don't know what you're talking about.

Colin: Really. I expect Alex's lover, that author, doesn't know what I'm talking about, either. But I'm sure she'd love to.

Sandi: You're talking rubbish. I've got a boyfriend. And his name isn't Alex.

Colin: You're shagging Alex though. And the author hasn't got a clue, has she?

Sandi: Where are you getting this information from?

Colin: It's irrelevant. What matters, though, is that J.K.Rowling isn't going to be very happy when she hears you've been whipping your panties off for her boyfriend. And I happen to have her mobile number.

Sandi: Are you trying to blackmail me?

Colin: Not at all....look, Sandi, you're gorgeous, I like you. I think we've got off on the wrong foot. I'd like to take you to dinner. Have a few drinks, go back to mine. Square the circle. The author need never find out about you and this *Alex*. I've heard she *knows* people. You know, *underworld* people. You really don't want to be messing with *her*.

Sandi: You're off your fucking nut you *arsehole*. And you *are* trying to blackmail me.

Colin: It's you who's using words like that, not me.

Sandi: Well, whatever you're doing, it stinks. You know nothing about me or my life.

Colin: So why are your hands shaking?

Sandi glances down at her hands and notices that the hand holding her plastic cup is, indeed, trembling. This utter, utter cunt. She doesn't know what to do.

Sandi: I don't know who's been saying what, but this is just gossip. My life is private.

Colin: So you didn't go back to his place on Friday night, then? Because that's what I've been told. And I know people who would love to get their hands on that information.

Sandi: You're unbelievable. And you're a fucking idiot for believing whatever shit people chat in your ear. You go and say what the hell you like to whoever you like, you know nothing about me, *nothing! Do you understand me?*

Sandi walks away from Colin, out of the Boom Boom Room and over to the table where her friend Gemma is crossing off names from the guest list. Sandi can feel tears pricking at her eyes as she walks towards Gemma, who is bent over the piece of paper, pencil in hand, her jet-black hair piled on top of her head and secured with a hair clip in the shape of a spear, her cobalt blue kimono shimmering in the brightly coloured lights from the bar.

Gemma looks up at Sandi and grins, red lipstick, glinting earrings, big almond eyes.

Gemma: Sandi! Leaving so soon?

Sandi: I might do…there's a bloke in there…he's just being a cunt…look, it's a great do, Gemma, it's not a reflection on you…

Gemma: Which one?

Sandi: Pink shirt. Moustache. I can see him from here. Talking to that bunch of women over there.

Gemma: What   did   he   do,   exactly?

Sandi: He's trying to blackmail me. Over something personal he thinks he's found out about me. Which is a load of fucking rubbish.

Gemma: What? Who does he work for?

Sandi: Ogilvy and Mather. He's one of their art directors.

Gemma: I've got friends there. What's his name?

Sandi: Colin. Colin Farmer. I met him at that Loophole opening a few months ago. Or, rather, he was harassing me before I was rescued by a mate…

Gemma speed-dials a number on her iPhone.

Gemma: Hi darls, it's me. Just wondering, what do you know about Colin Farmer?…OK…right…yeah…oh really? (laughing)… no…ah, right…oh god, no…you're kidding…really? Oh god that's awful, what a prat…yeah…listen, thanks for telling me… Ok. Thanks babes, we'll catch up next week, yeah? Hostessing tonight…

Gemma punches the phone off and looks at Sandi, evenly.

Gemma: He's a right cunt, apparently. Told a pack of lies about a mate of mine. Who got sacked over it.

Sandi: Sounds like him.

Gemma: You want to get your own back on him?

Sandi: How? He's freaked me out, actually…

Gemma: I picked these up from the printer's for a shoot we're doing tomorrow. I can spare one of them, I've got loads.

Gemma reaches into a voluminous leather bag and pulls out a stack of booklets. She hands one to Sandi. On the front it says 'Living With Sexually Transmitted Disease - Your Coping Guide.'

Gemma: Walk over to him and hand him one, making sure the other women see it. Tell him he just dropped it.

Sandi: I don't know…I don't want to make him angry…

Gemma: Hold on, Gary'll do it. Gazza! Would you do me a favour, darling? The bloke over there, with the moustache and pink shirt, he dropped this on the way in, would you give it to him? I don't want to move from here as people are still coming in. He was leering at me as well, fancies himself. Make sure those women he's talking to see the cover…

Gary, who's wearing a fitted shirt with contrasting cowboy-style collar and yoke and sporting a huge, bushy black beard, grins at Gemma then bursts out laughing as he notices the title of the pamphlet.

Gary: He dropped this? Really?

Sandi: Just give it to him, darls. He's a cunt.

Gary: OK darling.

Gemma and Sandi watch as Gary walks across the Boom Boom Room holding aloft the pamphlet, then stops at the edge of Colin's group and ostentatiously hands him the pamphlet.

Gary: You just dropped this, mate.
Colin: That's got nothing to do with me.
Gary: Ha! Not what I heard, buddy.

Gary elbows Colin in the side, and laughing, walks out of the Boom Boom Room again.

The women start looking at one another, then, obviously embarrassed, all imperceptibly glide away from him, like a shoal of fish into the shadows.

Colin, looking visibly angry, starts looking around him in all directions, not noticing Sandi and Gemma watching him from the main bar.

Sandi: Thanks…he looks furious.
Gemma: He won't bother you again…

Sandi can feel the tears bursting from her eyes now and rolling down her cheeks. Gemma puts her pen down and throws her arms around Sandi.

Gemma: Darling. Don't let him ruin your evening. Go to the bog, have a good cry, freshen up and whilst you're gone I'll get you a great big fuck off Mojito Amor. Then you can come back out here and help me with the guest list. You can be my co-hostess for the evening. Fuck him.
Sandi: OK. Thanks Gemma.

On the way to the toilets, a bloke in a mustard coloured frock coat bumps into Sandi accidentally and doesn't apologise. Sandi turns on her heels and walks straight for the exit door glancing at Gemma on her way out, who's laughing and chatting with a newly arrived group of guests. Sandi's had enough.

A Passion for Classic Cars

23

FRIGILIANA

fter almost an hour's drive, the airport taxi leaves the motorway and heads off up towards the mountains. In the distance Kate can see a white village, nestled in the hillside. She feels more and more at peace the closer they get to the village. Eventually the taxi emerges from the winding access road into the town square, above which sits the village itself, a labyrinth of narrow, cobbled streets and alleyways lined with white houses decorated with brightly coloured Moorish ceramics and red and pink geraniums tumbling down the walls.

Frigiliana's beauty, isolation and stunning surroundings, miles and miles of open landscape as far as the eye can see, bely its bloody history, when hundreds of years ago the local Moorish women threw themselves off the top of the old fort at the top of the village, rather than being captured by the Christians.

To Kate though, this village represents freedom and tranquillity. Already she can feel her family problems disappear over the horizon of her life, out of sight. She no longer cares about any of them, they can just get on with it. She glances at Christina, who's staring out of the window, smiling, and notices how plump and pink her lips look. Kate gets an overwhelming urge to lean over and kiss her, but the taxi draws to a halt suddenly and the driver turns round and addresses them both.

'We arrive. We here. Frigiliana. Beautiful mountain village for lovely English ladies.'

Just off the street is a narrow cobbled pathway, completely enclosed on all three sides by white-washed buildings, at the end of which is a blue door. The pathway is lined with palms and aloe veras and filled with hot sunshine from above. Kate feels like she's arrived in heaven. Fuck her mother. Fuck Alex. Fuck Matt. Fuck the lot of them.

Inside, the house is decorated in traditional Andalusian style, with brown terracotta tiled floors, white-washed walls and shutters on all the windows. The girls carry their trolleys into the double bedroom upstairs. It has one large, double bed and French windows. Christina rushes over and opens them to see the view. Part of the reason she was so looking forward to coming here was to take photographs, after all. Beyond the French windows is not a balcony, but an entire terrace, about thirty foot square, overlooking the old village of Frigiliana and the landscape beyond. The low walls of the terrace are lined with cacti, in the corner sits a small wrought iron table with two wicker chairs and in the centre of the terrace are two large foam mats spread out under the sun for sunbathing.

Kate joins Christina outside and they both stand there looking at the view, silenced by its beauty.

The terrace is overlooked only by a couple of houses opposite, which both have the shutters down so must currently be empty. Brilliant. Total privacy.

'It's private. We can sunbathe naked, Christina!' squeals Kate.

'We will...' smiles Christina. Later. Let's explore first...

Trudging up and down the steep, winding paths of the village exhausts Kate within an hour. She didn't think this was going to be a walking holiday. Christina, meanwhile, is obsessively taking photographs of everything. The olive-skinned locals, quietly sitting in doorways, watching the world go by, the ceramic wall-plaques describing the story of Frigiliana's violent past, the abundance of brightly-coloured flowers and ceramics which seem to overflow from every wall, nook and cranny.

Kate just wants to sunbathe. And the feeling of arousal which started in the taxi, watching Christina's lips, has not left her but now grown into an ache in her groin which won't go away.

'I think I'm just going back to the house, Christina. I fancy just chilling out. I'm knackered after the journey. I'll see you back there. I'll be on the terrace...'

'OK babes. Be there in an hour or so.'

Kate retraces her steps down the steep cobbled paths to their holiday house, walks upstairs grabbing a bottle of sun tan lotion and a bottle of water from the fridge on the way, flings open the French windows, pulls her t-shirt, shorts, knickers and sandals off and throws herself sulkily onto the foam mat. She glugs some water, then opens the bottle of lotion and rubs it all over her body, starting at her shoulders, rubbing it into her slender arms, then down over her body, the small, firm mounds of her breasts, the hard buds of her nipples, down over her flat stomach, then all over her legs, smearing the white liquid into her skin, down to her feet then back up the inside of her legs to her thighs, where she finishes off by brushing the tips of her greasy fingers over her mound of pubic hair, before laying down, stretching out and finally feeling the glorious hot sun on her naked skin.

She shuts her eyes and her mind starts to drift. Back to the long night she spent with Christina, yet to be repeated. She imagines Christina kissing her all over her body, licking between her legs, parting the folds of her pussy with her lips and massaging her clitoris with her tongue. She feels unbearable aroused, but wants to wait for Christina's return. The sun dances in patterns behind her closed eyelids, sweat forms on her brow and Kate sinks into a deep sleep.

Suddenly she awakes. Her eyes lazily open and her view is

filled with Christina's face, beaming down at her with a broad smile. An hour must have passed. She's back.

Christina has straddled Kate and sits above her, naked but for a sarong casually wrapped around her body.

'You've finished taking photographs?' asks Kate.

'For now.' smiles Christina.

As she languidly reaches over to grasp the water bottle, her full breasts move under the thin, chiffon material of the sarong. Kate is transfixed. Christina takes a swig of water and grins at Kate mischievously.

'Are you staring at my breasts?' she asks, teasingly.

'Yes' replies Kate. 'You're beautiful.'

Kate reaches up and slides a hand under the front centre parting in the sarong and widens her palm in order to caress Christina's breast. She cups it in her hand and feels its weight, then runs her fingers over the skin until she reaches the nipple, a firm, brown stiff little nub pointing upwards. She caresses it, rubbing the nipple gently between her fingers so that Christina sighs with pleasure.

Christina reaches up and unfastens the single knot holding the sarong together, and it peels away from her, sliding onto the lounging mat.

Now she's sitting astride Kate completely naked.

'Have you been lying in the sun all this time?' asks Christina.

'I feel asleep.'

'You'll need a top up of cream. Here, I'll do it.' Christina reaches for the sun tan lotion and squirts a fat blob of the white liquid into her palm, then reaches down and starts to massage the cream into Kate's skin, starting at her shoulders, massaging it into her neck, down over her breasts, rubbing all around the small mounds so that they wobble gently in the sun.

She continues down over Kate's belly then smoothes the cream over Kate's hips, and wriggles down the mat so that she can reach Kate's legs.

As she wriggles her breasts bounce up and down gently. Kate wants to hold them, wants to bury her face in them, but Christina is out of reach, sliding cream up and down Kate's legs until she reaches her thighs.

She glances up at Kate coquettishly before slipping one hand between Kate's thighs and parting her legs. She massages the cream into Kate's pale skin, sensing how aroused this is making her. Then she bends down and buries her face in the thick bush of Kate's pubic hair, smelling her fragrance and rubbing her nose over the oily folds of skin of her pussy.

Kate moans and Christina sits up and straddles her once again. She reaches down and cups Kate's breasts in her hands, whilst moving her hips forwards and backwards over Kate's body, her pussy rubbing over Kate's pubic mound. Kate can feel how wet Christina is and feels so aroused now she can't bear it any more. She slides her hand down Christina's body, down over her stomach and gently fondles the curly dark hair of Christina's pubis before sliding her hand face down underneath Christina's pussy to reach her own.

Christina takes her lead and reaches her hand down to masturbate, still sitting astride Kate, still moving her hips back and forth over Kate's body.

Kate feels unbearably aroused now. Every time Christina moves, her heavy breasts bob up and down. Christina's eyes close in arousal and desire as she rubs the folds of skin around her clitoris with one hand, and manipulates one of Kate's nipples in the other.

Kate can feel her orgasm rapidly approaching, but keeps watching Christina, whose head is thrown back, lips parted and eyes closed, her body smearing up and down over Kate's.

❧❧❧

Alessandro's penis is becoming uncomfortable as it swells inside his shorts. He impatiently pulls the long cotton shorts down so they drop around his ankles and grasps his engorged cock with one hand whilst he adjusts the blinds to get a better view with the other.

And he thought Frigiliana was going to be dull as ditch water. He can barely contain his joy at the view from his apartment window. Two stunning hot lesbians masturbating together. And for free! He runs his free hand down over his tanned, bare chest, admiring the feel of his own taut, rippling muscles, as he vigorously pumps his penis back and forth with his other hand. God, the brunette with the big tits is wriggling around on the other one who's lying down. She's fucking gorgeous! They're both fucking gorgeous! He can barely contain himself. His cock has never felt so stiff. He glances down at the shaft, swollen and rock hard, the veins prominent and the bulbous head of his penis already glistening with pre-come as he massages it firmly and quickly, his pace quickening as he can feel his orgasm approaching.

❧❧❧

Christina cries out as she comes, flopping forward onto Kate and kissing her deeply on the lips, her tongue hungrily seeking out Kate's as their mouths merge in warmth and love. Her body arcs and bolts above Kate's as Kate in turn comes, wrapping her arms around Christina and clasping her tightly as her hips thrust up and down in passion. Finally, Christina buries her face in Kate's hair and lets out a long, slow sigh of relief from the release of sexual tension. The two of them lie still in the hot, early evening sun, their arms around one another.

❧❧❧

Thick, long, spurts of spunk fly out of the crimson tip of Alessandro's engorged penis, splashing against the white-washed wall of his room, as he cries out loud at the force of his orgasm. One of the girls raises her head and turns round, looking in Alessandro's direction. He quickly dives away from the blinds, even though there's no way he could be seen.

'Did you hear that?' asks Christina.

'What?'

'It sounded like someone grunting or something.'

'No, I didn't hear anything…'

'Up there. From that window…'

'Oh yeah…those blinds were shut when I came out here. They're half open now. So that house isn't empty after all…'

'You don't think some fucker's been watching us, do you?'

'Nah. Probably not.'

'Pervs.'

❧❧❧

The view of the rolling green slopes topped with the white mountain village at their crest like a snow-dusted mountain, is simply stunning. Kate and Christina both sit at a table on the terrace of Restaurante El Mirador, sipping Irish coffees and gazing into the distance, over the countryside to the sea beyond.

'I think I'm in heaven.' says Christina.

'So do I' murmurs Kate. 'This is just perfect. We made the right decision, coming over here, don't you think?'

Christina grins. 'Yup. We did.' She picks up her Nikon, adjusts the telephoto lens and starts taking pictures of the view.

A tall Mediterranean looking man in his mid-twenties approaches their table with a little boy lost look on his face.

'Hello…er… I am thinking can you help me with this map?' His confused look turns to a warm smile.

Alessandro is very, very good looking. Thick, straight dark brown hair which curls slightly at his collar, cleanly shaved and green eyes which crinkle at the corner when he smiles. He holds forward a map of Frigiliana.

'We've only just arrived ourselves, we don't know our way around, but sit down, we'll have a look.' says Christina, studying Alessandro carefully.

'Thank you. I only arrive today too and I leave tomorrow. I trying to find this shop which sells ceramica. For a plant pot. For my mother back in Italy.'

'Oh, you're Italian?' smiles Kate.

'Yes. I'm Alessandro. From Milano.' Alessandro raises his chin slightly, obviously proud of his home town.

'Hi Alessandro. I'm Christina. And this is Kate.' Christina gestures airily towards Kate sitting next to her. ' I love the Milan shows. The street fashion is to die for as well. I always get great shots at Milan Fashion Week.'

'Oh, you're a photographer?' asks Alessandro, looking at Christina intently.

'Yes.'

'And I'm a model.' announces Kate, archly.

Alessandro ignores her, continuing to look at Christina. 'Lei è quella con grandi ciocce che era in cima' he thinks.('She's the one with big tits who was on top.')

Christina notices his gaze and catches his eye, not looking away.

'Where are you staying?' she asks.

'Oh, nearby, just up the hill…' he answers, vaguely. 'And you two, where you stay?'

'Up the hill, too.' says Christina.

The air is crackling with electricity between Alessandro and Christina. Kate shifts uncomfortably on the warm metal of her chair.

'Yes. We're staying together.' Kate announces.

'Oh, to travel together, two girls, much safer.' answers Alessandro.

'It's not for safety. We're *together*.' says Kate, firmly.

'Together! Like a couple?' asks Alessandro, glancing at Kate then turning to Christina and smiling, warmly.

'Like a couple, that's right. We're lovers.' says Kate.

'Oh, I understand. Lovers. Lesbians, yes? Very sexy.'

Christina swigs her Irish coffee and looks at Alessandro intently over her cup. He's the first man she's seen since that twat Stefan whom she's actually found attractive.

Alessandro grins at Christina. 'Lesbians. They always change after they meet me. Another woman is not enough after they have been with Alessandro.'

'Is that right?' says Christina. 'And what do you have to offer that a woman doesn't?'

'Maybe it's something about us Italian men....'

Kate bursts out laughing. 'Really.'

'What is it about Italian men, then?' asks Christina.

'We like to give pleasure. Until the woman is too tired to beg for more. We give pleasure again and again and again.' Alessandro looks Christina in the eye as he's speaking and she doesn't look away. She leans forward slightly.

'So, you think you could, like, turn us? Is that it?'

'I don't understand...' says Alessandro, looking confused. Christina is as gobsmacked as Kate at his arrogance, but fuck he's hot.

'Turn us into a straight couple. Where we fancy men...'

Alessandro smiles mischievously. 'My map. I need to find ceramica shop for my mother.'

Kate's phone rings with the irritating tweety bird whistle tone which Christina has been asking her to change since they left London. Kate answers it.

'What? I'm on *fucking holiday*.' she says acidly, then holds the phone away from her and hisses at Christina 'Fucking Matt. What the fuck does *he* want?'

Christina and Alessandro both look at Kate blankly, as she starts shouting into the phone at Matt and stomps off from the table, striding away from the cafe and out of their earshot.

'We passed a lovely ceramics shop in the taxi on the way to our guest house, Alessandro.' says Christina in a syrupy voice. 'I can show you if you want. I'll leave a note for Kate to meet us back at our place, she'll be on the phone for ages if it's Matt.'

'Who's Matt?' he asks.

'Trouble back home.' says Christina ominously, then smiles. 'But we've come here to get away from that. We've come here to follow our dreams and have fun…' Christina grins openly at Alessandro and he grins back at her. Both look deeply into the other's eyes without looking away.

Christina leaves the money on the table for their coffees plus a tip, and walks away from the cafe with Alessandro. Kate is in the distance, her back turned to them, gesticulating with one hand whilst holding the phone in the other.

It's still early evening. The day trippers have gone and the locals are yet to emerge for evening meals and promenades in the balmy evening sun. The cobbled streets lined with white-washed houses are quiet apart from the hum of cicadas.

At the far end of the main street, Christina finds the shop she'd passed in the taxi, Artesania de Frigiliana, with its exterior wall covered in multi-coloured bright ceramic wall planters. But it's shut.

'You may have to come back later after siesta…' says Christina.

'I will. This looks perfect. Thank you, Christina.' says Alessandro, glancing at her and smiling warmly. Fuck, there's no two ways about it. He is Hot. Hot. Hot.

They both turn round simultaneously and begin walking up the hill again. A small cobbled road branches off to the right.

'I was going to have a walk round the village to take more photos. You're welcome to come with me if you like...' says Christina.

'I'd like that.' Alessandro says softly, smiling at her and looking into her eyes. Christina can feel herself melting. Almost against her will, her pussy is aching. She hasn't felt like this about a man for a long time.

The couple walk up the steep little side street, which then leads to another steep side street, all of them lined with white-washed houses covered in plant pots brimming over with bright, tumbling geraniums. Within minutes they are high up atop the village where the road peters out into a dirt track surrounded by cacti and shrubs. Behind them the houses recede into the distance and in front of them down the hill lies the stunning countryside, the sea beyond a shimmering blue plaque under a cloudless sky.

Christina stops to take some photos of the view, then turns and focuses her lens on Alessandro, who stands there looking steadily at her. The camera loves him, he is absolutely beautiful. As Christina moves the camera so his face is in the centre of the frame he smiles slightly and she captures a perfect shot.

'Gorgeous.' she says. Alessandro smiles again as she puts her camera in its bag. The sun is moving down towards the horizon, and sunset. Behind them stands the remains of an old house, now deserted.

'I want to photograph it.' announces Christina and walks towards the house and then round the back where an overgrown terrace is shaded by a cooling palm tree. Alessandro follows her and watches her as she runs her hands against the crumbling masonry of the back wall. She stops and turns to look at him. He fixes her with his eyes and strides towards her then stops in front of her. He peels the shoulder strap of her bag from her and gently lowers it to the ground, then stands up and cups her face in his hands.

'You are bellissima. You are like a goddess.' he says. 'The first time I saw you…' and he trails off, perfectly aware that Christina has no idea about the first time Alessandro saw her, naked, sitting astride Kate and rocking back and forth, her pussy rubbing against Kate's body until they both simultaneously came with Alessandro looking on, fervently and feverishly masturbating.

He pulls Christina towards him and kisses her on the mouth. She melts into him, he is a wonderful kisser, better than Kate. His lips feels full and soft, his tongue gentle and probing. Their bodies meld together as one as they hold each other, as if they were made to be together.

Time stands still as they kiss. Christina can feel her heart beating fast and her pussy aching unbearably. She pulls gently away from Alessandro and says

'Fuck me.'

Alessandro lifts Christina's short sun-dress and pulls her panties down. As she steps out of them he unbuckles the belt of his jeans and pulls them down. He's not wearing any underpants. His cock is standing stiffly upright. Christina is relieved that it's huge. She can't remember needing to be fucked as much as she feels at this moment. Alessandro pulls Christina towards him, puts one hand round the back of her neck and and kisses her deeply again, then with the other hand holds Christina's bottom, pulling her towards him. Christina guides Alessandro's penis into her and lifts herself up onto her toes to ease his penetration. As he thrusts his hips forward and pushes his penis all the way into her she cries out loud. He holds her bottom firmly with both hands now and begins thrusting into her, fucking her with fast, regular long strokes. Christina thrashes her head from side to side in ecstasy and feels herself coming. Her cries become louder as she loses all sense of where she is. All she's aware of is the heat and smell of Alessandro as he pumps his cock into her until eventually he cries out too and she can feel the floods of semen spurting deep inside her.

Alessandro holds her close as she slides back down onto the soles of her feet, her arms still wrapped around him, his penis slipping out of her.

He looks at her, caressing her hair gently as she looks at him, and her heart bursts with desire.

Christina hadn't intended this to happen. This was meant to be a joyful, impetuous and meaningless fuck.

Shit.

24

REVELATIONS

olin approaches the 1960s block of flats with suspicion.

'This visit to Matt is a complete waste of his time, but the arrogant fuck has had it coming, ever since he stole Kate from me eighteen months ago. Yes, Kate was married to that absolute pillock Alex at the time we were going out, but that was a complete farce as well as this ridiculous diversion with the dumb model. She does have this uncanny ability to pick complete tossers for boyfriends. Good job I'm still around to advise her.' thinks Colin, straightening his blazer collar as he peers amongst the bells for Kate's flat number. 3-5a. That's her. Seeing as she's in Spain, Colin will have Matt to himself, without Kate getting all defensive.

The buzzer sounds and a voice on the other end says

'Yup?'

'It's Colin. We met a while ago. Kate's ex. I've got some information for you which I think you'll want to know.'

'Fuck, man. I'm in the middle of something. Just spit it out. What is it?'

'That's not how I roll, bud. I'm offering you the helicopter view here. You need to get all your ducks in a row...'

'Right. Come on up then if it's so important. Take the lift on your left. Floor 3 then second door on the right.'

'Bingo.'

Colin stands outside door 5a impatiently drumming his fingers against his iPhone case. Matt opens the door, looking dishevelled. Colin looks him up and down, disparagingly.

'Late start?'

'It's my day off. So…what is it you've travelled all the way to Hemel Hempstead to tell me?'

'Dunno where to start, really, pal. Just thought I'd take the lead and champion some key issues. Shall I come in?'

'No. I'm busy.'

'Yeah, you look it. Alright, we'll start with Kate. She's in Spain.'

'I know. What business is it of yours?'

Colin chuckles smarmily.

'She hasn't told you? We still see one another now and then. When she's bored.'

'Really.'

'…wanna know who she's in Spain with?'

'Not really.'

'Her girlfriend. Christina. Big tits? Gorgeous? They're fucking. Kate's decided she's a rug muncher.'

'Look if you've come here to gossip, I'm really not interested. And I still can't see what it's got to do with you, anyway.'

'Kate's a good friend of mine. She needs protecting. Her business is my business. So it's got everything to do with me, and, pal, it should be on your agenda too. Considering you're fucking her mother.'

'I dunno what you're talking about, mate, but you've got the wrong end of the stick.'

'Nah, pal, I haven't. I haven't got any wrong end of any fucking stick. I'm talking about Gigi. Your girlfriend, right?'

Matt stares at Colin, blankly, wishing the prat would just fuck off from his doorstep.

'Only her name isn't Gigi' continues Colin, his lips curling into a sneer as he spits the words out. 'Her real name's *Julia*.'

Matt says nothing, just stares at Colin...

'She's *Julia*. The *author*. *Kate's mother*. You've been fucking *Kate's mother*, mate.'

Matt can feel his stomach tighten with fear and panic but doesn't want to betray his feelings to this cunt Colin so continues to stare at him stonily.

'Just fuck off, Colin. You don't know what the fuck you're talking about. And my life has got fuck all to do with you anyway.'

'Ah but it has, pal, it has. Because Kate and I are still like *that*.' Colin links the fingers of both his hands together and shakes them up and down, vigorously.

'And Kate's obviously not very happy about about this latest chain of events. Especially as you ain't the first, mate. Kate's mother's got a habit of shagging all the men in her life because she is a batshit crazy dried-up old bird desperate for attention and a shag.'

Despite his shock and fear, something inside Matt snaps at this description of the woman he loves so much. He punches Colin square on the nose, instantly making his nose bleed.

Colin squawks with pain and reaches up to protect his nose, realising it's bleeding and holding his hand away from his face to examine the blood.

'That's assault!' he squeaks in a high voice.

'Just fuck off.' says Matt, wearily, and slams the door shut on Colin, who continues to stare at the door in front of his face, even after it's been slammed shut.

Matt walks back into his flat and returns to his balcony, where he rests his hands on the rail and stares down at them. He's never punched someone in the face before in his entire life. It actually feels good.

Julia. Julia. Julia. Gigi is gone. Julia is in his life, now. And she's Kate mother. His heart sinks, and then he looks out into the trees beyond and thinks

'Fuck it. I love her. They can both fuck off, Kate and Colin. They don't matter. All that matters is Julia.' And then he says her name out loud, trying it on for size.

'Julia. Julia. Julia.'

❧❧❧

Alex walks into the office looking furtive and sheepish. It's the first time Sandi has seen him since they slept together. He walks up to her, dumps his bag down and smiles.

Sandi: You missed that networking do last night, have you been ill or something?

Alex: Yeah. Must have come down with something.

Sandi: Right.

Alex: Look. About Friday night…

Sandi: It's fine, Alex. Just forget it…

Alex: No, Sandi, hear me out. Look. I was really, really pissed.

Sandi: I know.

Alex: That's not why I came back to yours.

Sandi: Yes, I know…

Alex: I just don't want it to be awkward…

Sandi: It won't be.

Alex: Fine…

Sandi: There's something you should know, though. Somehow, that dickhead I told you about a few months ago, Colin Farmer, you know, the one that turned out to be Kate's ex…

Alex: Yeah, him. Total dick…

Sandi: Well I don't know how he's found out, but he knows about us. I presume through Kate. Somehow. So Kate must know, too…

Alex: I see…

Sandi: And he threatened to tell Julia unless I went to dinner with him and then back to his….

Alex: He fucking *what?* What a fucking *cunt!* If I'd been there I'd have decked him!

Sandi: But you weren't there, were you. You were…'ill'…or avoiding me. Or whatever.

Alex: I wasn't avoiding you. What a cunt.

Sandi: So the point is, I think we should tell Julia. About us. Before he does. Because I made it clear I wasn't going to give in to his demands.

Alex: No. No fucking way. She doesn't have to know. It was a one-off.

Sandi: I see. I was a 'one-off'. That's nice, Alex.

Alex: I don't mean it like that. I mean…look, I was drunk, I just told you. I'm sorry about Colin, but I don't think we should do or say anything right at this moment. Julia will go batshit crazy. I can't deal with it…

Sandi: Right. You can't deal with it.

Alex: Correct.

Alex marches off to the bathroom, leaving his mobile on the computer table. Sandi picks it up and scrolls through until she finds Julia's number. She walks out of the office and onto the street outside, ringing the number.

Sandi: Julia?

Julia: Um…who is this? This is Alex's phone…

Sandi: Hi Julia. My name's Sandi. I work with Alex.

Julia: Oh, hello. Yes, I've heard all about you.

Sandi: Well…I don't know what you've heard…

Julia: It doesn't matter. What can I do for you? Is everything OK? Is Alex OK?

Sandi: Julia, I'm not proud of this. But there's something I think you should know, because if I don't tell you, someone else will, and I think it's better coming from me...

Julia: Go on...

Sandi: Alex and I slept together last Friday.

Julia: Oh...

Sandi: We went out for a drink after work. Alex was very drunk. I don't think it would have happened, otherwise.

Julia: Well that's OK, then...

Sandi: Look, none of it's OK. And I'm sorry. He was really, really drunk...

Julia: Which explains his gargantuan hangover when I got back on Saturday...

Sandi: It was a huge mistake...

Julia: I see...

Sandi: A 'one-off'...

Julia: A 'one-off'. Right.

Sandi: And to be honest, it was a joke...

Julia: And that explains why I'm standing here in my kitchen splitting my sides with laughter.

Sandi: I *mean* that it was a bit...pathetic. Don't go getting any ideas that we were hanging from the chandeliers...

Julia: I wasn't getting any ideas.

Sandi: Because it was crap, to be honest. He nearly passed out straight away.

Julia: Sandi, much as I'm sure you find this absorbing, I'm really not interested in the details about you having sex with my partner.

Sandi: Julia, please. I'm trying to do the right thing. I'm trying to be honest. I feel terrible about what we did.

Julia: Well, I'm sure you can sort it out. In fact, you can sort it out round at your place, if you want. Because Alex will be moving out of mine pronto.

Sandi: Don't you think that's a bit…er…rash?

Julia: No, I don't think it's a bit 'rash'. I think it's the sensible option, frankly.

Sandi: Well, he's very good-looking. You don't often come across men like him. And so much younger than yourself…

Julia: He's a bit old for me actually, sweetie. You're welcome to him.

Julia cuts the phone call off and sighs, heavily. Brilliant. Now she doesn't feel guilty. What a lovely, harmonious weight off her mind.

25

DECISIONS

hristina returns to the guest house at dusk. Everything is quiet. She walks upstairs, into the bedroom and towards the French doors, open to the terrace beyond. Kate is standing on the terrace with her back turned, looking at the view. She turns round when she hears Christina and glugs back the remains of a large glass of white wine.

Kate: Where have you been? Your phone's been switched off! You've been gone nearly two hours!

Christina: It ran out of battery and I...I kind of lost track of the time, sorry.

Kate: You lost track of the *time?* What were you *doing?*

Christina: Well, I was just wandering around taking photos...

Kate: I see.

Christina: I don't like the tone of your voice, Kate. You're making me feel like I've done something wrong.

Kate: Well you haven't been very considerate, have you? Here we are just arrived on holiday after I've had a completely shit time in England and the very first evening you just fuck off somewhere with some bloke and stop answering your phone!

Christina. I told you. I ran out of battery. And it wasn't 'some bloke'. He's called *Alessandro*.

Kate: I know. He introduced himself. Have you been with him the whole time? For two hours?

Christina: Well, actually…yes. I have.

A look of thunder passes over Kate's face as she feels an acidic knot of jealousy burn her stomach.

Kate: What do you mean?

Christina: I mean yes, I've been with Alessandro for the last couple of hours.

Kate: What, it took you two frigging hours to show him where some pottery shop was?

Christina: No. It took us two hours to fuck.

Kate stands looking at Christina in utter disbelief. Christina reaches towards the patio table and coolly pours herself a glass of wine from the bottle which Kate has put in an ice bucket to chill.

Kate: You fucking what? You've fucked him?

Christina: Yeah. I did. It just happened.

Kate: What, you stood there looking at his map, said 'Oh look here's the pottery shop so you can buy your mum some mugs' and then he gets his dick out and shags you in the doorway?

Christina: Not quite like that, no. And they're not pottery shops. They're ceramic shops.

Kate: Oh for fuck's sake Christina, who gives a shit what they're called? So where did you fuck him then?

Christina: Does it really matter?

Kate: Yes!

Christina: We went for a walk to the top of the village. It was just something…spontaneous…

Kate: I thought you'd gone off men!

Christina: Well, obviously I haven't.

Kate: So I'm not good enough then…

Christina: It's got nothing to do with you. We just clicked…

Kate: So how did he shag you? Lying down? Standing up?

Christina: I'm not going into this. It happened. That's that.

Kate: No, I want to know! Tell me!

Christina: No, Kate, I've told you enough! This has turned into a horrible, ugly scene. I didn't come on holiday for this!

Kate: Oh, so you think I did?

Christina: We came away to have fun. And that's what I've been doing.

Kate: At my fucking expense! Well you can get out, go on, just fuck off to his place, go and stay with him, see if I care.

Christina finishes her glass of wine and smiles, sweetly. 'I think I will.'

❧❧❧

Christina quickly throws the few things she's already unpacked into her suitcase and silently leaves the house. Kate sits on the terrace, weeping. After ten minutes of feeling sorry for herself and wondering why the world has turned against her, she rings Colin. She can always depend on Colin…

Colin: Babes. How's Spain?

Kate: Terrible. You'll never believe what's happened… Christina…never mind I'll fill you in later…just come out here, can you, Colin? I've got the apartment to myself for the next 6 days…'

Colin: I can't babes. I've godda sunset this Fiat campaign and square the circle on the key deliverables.

Kate: What? What Fiat campaign?

Colin: I must have told you about it, babes. If I can just drill down this week I'll be on it like a car bonnet.

Kate: You mean you don't want to come…

Colin: It's not you, babes. It's me.

Kate: Too fucking right, Colin. I need you right now and you're just being fucking selfish, thinking of work, work work!

Colin: Babes, you're trying to tangibilise the intangible…

Kate: What does that even *mean* Colin! I'm just trying to get you to jump on a fucking plane! How hard can it be?

Colin: Your anger isn't incentivising me, Kate. We're not singing from the same hymn sheet here, are we?

Kate: Colin! I'm fucking upset! Christina's turned out to be a *total slut!*

Colin: Really? Now we're talking…

Kate: Don't be fucking *ridiculous,* Colin! She's shat on me!

Colin: Not really into scat, babes.

Kate: I don't mean literally you idiot. I mean she's been off fucking some Italian bloke!

Colin: Ah, so she doesn't only drink from the furry cup, she likes a nosh of pork sword as well. There's hope for me yet!

Kate: For fuck's sake, Colin, I'm asking you for help! I want to come out here and rescue me!

Colin: Much as the idea of jetting out to the Costa del Sol for some pussy sandwich is tempting, I've got key deliverables to meet, I told you.

Kate: I don't fucking give a shit about your key fucking deliverables, I need you here!

Colin: Babes, you're not giving me any leverage, here. You're pushing me to get on the bus together and go to the seaside with this idea, but I can't.

Kate: You know what, Colin? Why don't you just *stuff your key deliverables up your arse and fuck off!*

Decisions

❧❧❧

'It is very near Calle Alta, ring me when you get here.' says Alessandro, warmly.

'I'm here already! That's right behind our place!' says Christina.

Christina checks Google maps on her fully charged phone.

'Villa Sebastian Bach. That's it, right in front of me!'

'I come to the door and you come inside.'

Alessandro opens the door and stands there, leaning slightly against the door post, a white towel lazily wrapped around his waist, his upper torso bare and tanned, a huge grin plastered across his face.

'You come back for more Alessandro. I like that.'

'Just let me in, you goof-ball' says Christina, grinning back at him.

She brushes past him running one hand lightly down the firm ripples of muscles on his stomach.

'You are, quite simply, divine. An Italian angel.'

'I know.' coos Alessandro, smugly.

Alessandro's apartment is two floors up. Christina walks in through the open door of the lounge whilst Alessandro follows her, watching her bottom move against the thin, black chiffon of her sarong as she moves and already longing to remove it so that he can fuck her again.

Christina drops her bag onto the sofa and walks over to the open window. The view is mostly of rooftops, but just down below is a terrace with the already familiar sunbathing mats, cacti, wicker chairs and wrought-iron table at which sits Kate, yelling into the phone at someone.

Christina is riveted, from her slightly higher vantage point she can hear everything.

'Colin! I'm fucking upset! Christina's turned out to be a *total slut!*'

Oh. So *that's* how it is, is it? Friendship over, then. Suddenly Christina is filled with a dreadful thrill. If she can now so clearly see Kate, then it means Alessandro could, possibly have seen her and Kate earlier on. Not only seen, but been actually *watching* them.

Christina turns slightly as Alessandro wraps his arms around her from behind and slides his hands beneath the stretchy fabric of her bikini top, finding her stiff little nipples and caressing them with his fingers.

He moves his body closer to hers until he is pressed right against her, holding her tightly. He muzzles her ear with his mouth and whispers,

'She is a very angry Kate, yes?'

'She just called me a slut, but fuck her…'

Alessandro lifts the black chiffon of Christina's sarong and peels down her bikini bottoms. Still nuzzling her neck with his soft lips, he parts the towel around his waist slightly so reveal his penis, swollen and jutting out towards Christina's bottom. He moves even closer and she can smell the heavy, sweet scent of his warm skin and the hardness of his cock brushing against her. He guides his penis towards her pussy and enters her from behind. She gasps out loudly and he slides his hand back up her body and then clasps her full, heavy breasts in both hands as he proceeds to gently pump into her. Christina's lips part with desire and she throws her head back slightly to allow Alessandro full access to slide his tongue up and down the warm skin of her neck and then gently nibble her ear-lobes as all the time he keeps up a rhythmic pumping of his cock which makes Christina feels she's going to explode with heat and longing.

The sight of Kate just below them angrily screaming into her phone, unaware of her former lover being fucked right in front of her a few dozen feet away, makes Christina unbearably excited.

Alessandro increases the speed of his fucking her, moving in and out of her oily pussy with long, firm thrusts of his stiff penis. The movement of Christina's breasts bouncing around in his hands is driving him crazy and he can feel his orgasm rising up in an unstoppable surge. Christina trembles with the heat of her own, overcome with lust, desire and an incessant need for her new lover and the deep gratifying feeling of his cock inside of her. As Alessandro comes he cries out in passion as he spurts thick streams of spunk deep inside Christina's pussy. Her legs buckle and he clasps her hips to keep inside her, unaware of anything else around him.

The world has receded into nothingness and erotic mist as Christina is overcome with the dream-like furnace of her orgasm, so that when she floats back down to earth from the sexual cloud which transported her away, all she can see is the empty terrace before her.

She has no idea whether Kate saw or heard them fucking, which fills Christina with a kind of exuberant dread...

26

THE FRENCH HOUSE, SOHO

he French House is once again a tranquil afternoon retreat after the hustle and bustle of Soho. A small group of casually dressed twenty-something Bohemians stand on the far right of the bar, deep in earnest discussion. Two elderly men sit at a table silently staring into space, sipping at glasses of wine.

After buying a small, cold glass of Hoegaarden, Matt sinks into a seat in the corner, under the pictures of French heroes lining the walls. He takes a sip of beer and a feeling of peace and contentment spreads through his body. His entire life suddenly seems to be falling into place. So Gigi is Julia is Kate's mother. So fucking what? He loves her. That's all that matters. And soon she'll be here.

A brunette with hair tumbling over her face in tendrils sits at the bar drinking a glass of red wine and laughing with her companion, a middle-aged bloke with a heavily-lined face. As if they sense Matt watching, the bloke turns round, catches Matt's eye and half smiles, vaguely, as though he's thinking about something else. His eyes are penetrating, alight and full of warmth. The woman elbows him in the rib area of his black leather jacket and creases up laughing again as she points at something on her iPhone.

She's beautiful and charismatic and her face seems annoyingly familiar. Has he met her before? Suddenly it hits him. It's the actress, Helena Bonham Carter.

Mixing in the circles he does and unimpressed by fame or beauty, he's nevertheless intrigued by the couple's charisma as she continues to laugh and he exudes a bemused languid acceptance of life and all its quirks and foibles.

Matt looks away, not wanting to be seen to stare and then notices the door of the pub open and Julia walking in. She's wearing a figure-hugging cornflower blue dress, her hair is up in a sixties-style bun on top of her head and her breasts look magnificent as she swings through the door, grinning at him, before striding straight over to him.

He stands up and wraps his arms around her, burying his face in her neck before kissing her gently on the lips in greeting.

'You look gorgeous.'

'So do *you*.' she answers.

'I got you a glass of wine…'

'Thanks.'

Julia sits down beside him and grins.

'I've missed you. And it's only been three days. Insane.'

'Julia…'

Julia's face falls as she studies Matt's and the concerned look passing over it.

'What is it?'

Matt audibly takes a deep breath.

'What? Tell me!' insists Julia.

'I know who you are. I know that yer Kate's mother.'

Julia's face seems to cave inwards with shock and guilt.

'Oh.God. Right…'

'How long did yer think you could keep this up? Why didn't yer tell me?'

'I don't know. I'm sorry. I'm *sorry*, Matt. I didn't mean to lie. But remember at Stef's you told me you were a plumber and I told you I was an artist? Then you came clean and admitted you were a model? Well I knew then that you *had* to be Kate's boyfriend. I mean how many gorgeous blonde curly-haired male models called Matt live in Hemel Hempstead? It was a no-brainer. And then I realised that if I told you I was really called Julia and I was an author, you'd likely go down the very same road of deduction as I had. How many authors called Julia live in Tewin? I'm sorry. But I didn't want you to put two and two together and realise I was Kate's mother. You might have run a mile. I just didn't want to risk it, guilty as I felt...'

'You're right, I probably *would* have run a mile.'

'Quite. Look, I've hated lying, especially as we've grown so close...'

Julia reaches out and holds Matt's hand.

'I'd fallen too far to risk having to crawl out on my own, Matt. I knew I'd have to tell you soon. I was a coward. I was putting it off...'

Matt looks at Julia with warmth and love in his eyes and squeezes her hand.

'Kate and I are finished anyroad. Right now she's off in Spain somewhere fucking some photographer woman..'

'Really? You're kidding? How do you know?

'Her twat of an ex, Colin, paid me a visit at home yesterday and told me. I didn't want to talk about it on the phone, I wanted to tell you in person...'

'Very considerate, thank you. So, what, Kate's decided she's a *lesbian?*'

'No idea what's going through her head.'

'She didn't tell me anything about this. Mothers are always the first to be blamed and the last to be told. Typical.'

'Well, the point is, I don't fucking care what she's doing. Kate and I are history. I love *you*, Julia.'

'I love you too, Matt.'

Matt leans over and kisses Julia gently on the lips and she pulls away, smiling at him.

'We'll have to find somewhere to go after this…' she whispers.

'Too right.'

Matt takes another swig of his beer and Julia calmly takes a sip of her wine, glancing away from the table and out of the strange, revelatory bubble in which she's been engrossed.

'Fuck. That's Bruce Robinson at the bar!'

'Who?'

'He wrote *Withnail and I*' murmurs Julia. 'I adore him. Shit, I've always wanted to meet him.'

'Well go and tap Helena Bonham Carter on the shoulder and ask if she minds you having a natter, then.' laughs Matt.

'Is that? Helena Bonham Carter? Oh yeah! It is! Fuck! Helena Bonham Carter and Bruce Robinson. Sitting at the bar in The French House!'

Julia looks suddenly crestfallen. 'But I can't just go and *introduce myself*. It's not the right time. You find out I'm your girlfriend's mother and I start chatting to *Bruce Robinson*. It's just too surreal.'

'Go and say hello. He looks like a decent bloke to me. He won't mind.'

'People come to The French House in order not to be bothered. They don't want gushing fans with the sparkling gaze of wonder plastered all over their slack-jawed faces. I *hate* it when fans recognise me.'

'You fucking *love* it. Go and talk to him. It's probably the only chance you'll ever get. What if he drops dead next week of a heart attack and you missed your chance? You'll never forgive yourself.'

'I'll say something on the way out, then he won't feel trapped.'

'Well we're going now. Because I need to fuck you, Gigi.'

'Julia.'

'You'll always be Gigi to me, Julia.'

Julia smiles at Matt, gracious beyond his years, just one of the many reasons she loves him. She finishes off her drink, stands and picks up her bag.

Helena collapses into fits of giggles at something Bruce has obviously just said to her. Julia doesn't want to interrupt them.

'Go. On.' insists Matt, grinning.

The couple walk over to the bar. Bruce and Helena look at them with half smiles on their faces.

'Hi Bruce, you don't know me, but my name's Julia. I just wanted to say how much I enjoyed your novel, *The Peculiar Memories of Thomas Penman*...'

Bruce raises his eyebrows and smiles.

'Not many people mention *that* one.'

'Well I loved it.'

'She's too modest to say, but she's an author too.' says Matt, smiling warmly.

Helena leans forward slightly, her brows furrowing as she studies Matt.

'Aren't you in those *ads* for *H&M?*'

'Well, they're doing quite a big campaign at the moment. I'm only in one of the ads...' says Matt, embarrassed.

'I *thought* I recognised you. Plastered across the fucking tube, Bruce, have you seen the ads?

'Can't say that I can quite recall them, no.'

'*Love* your work, darling. 'coos Helena to Matt.

'Um, thanks.'

'I've seen you at one of Stella's parties too. 'continues Helena, coquettishly.

'Who the fuck is Stella? What is this? A who's who of fucking London?' interjects Bruce.

'Stella McCartney, silly.' laughs Helena. 'One of my *favourite* designers.'

Bruce takes a swig of his wine. 'Whado I know? I never go to parties. Avoid them like the plague. I live the life of a *recluse*.'

'Oh shut up and stop being so self-pitying, yer wanker.' teases Helena.

'I'm not being self-pitying! I deliberately avoid going to that sort of shit, you know that. Nothing against your mate Stella, of course.'

'I don't like 'em either, love.' says Matt.

'When Matt met me, he told me he was a plumber!' laughs Julia.

'Do you know, I need a good plumber. Can you really, *plumb?*' asks Helena, intrigued.

'Aye, ah can.'

'Oh! You're a *Northerner!* exclaims Helena, delightedly. 'How quaint! I love the way you all talk so...so...*Shakespearean!* 'Thou' and 'thee'. It's so *resonant* and *evocative!*'

'I am indeed a Northerner. From Yorkshire, God's Own County. And now I'm going to fuck the woman I love, so...nice to meet ya both.'

'Oh *do* have fun! Lovely to meet you, *bye!*' trills Helena, her laughter rippling through The French House as she waves her hand in a way that manages to be simultaneously dismissive and affectionate.

Bruce smiles at Julia and Julia smiles back at Bruce, before she walks from one life into another.

27

TANYA AND THE BLOKE WITH THE BEARD AT THE BFI CAFE II

anya gently takes her mochaccino latte out onto the terrace of the BFI cafe and sits down at the one remaining free table, alone. The sweltering heat of the past few days is passing, the temperature has dropped slightly and a cool, refreshing breeze is ruffling over from the direction of the Thames, whilst the sun is still hot enough to warm Tanya's face as she sighs with contentment at this little island of tranquillity in an otherwise hectic day.

Her iPhone pings. It's a message from Kate.

having a fucking awful time in Spain, will tell you when I see you babes xxx

Tanya suddenly misses her friend, realising that it's no fun going for a coffee without her. She stares out towards the Thames, wondering what calamity has descended on Kate now. Her life seems to be a string of one disaster after another.

'Excuse me, do you mind if I sit here? I can't find a free table...'

Tanya looks up at the stranger hovering by her table. Fuck! Fuck fuck fuck! It's the bloke with the beard! The one who was here last time, typing up his stupid book, 'How I Learnt to Understand Women.'!

'Course not.' says Tanya, coolly taking a sip of her coffee.

The bloke, who still has a beard, only it's even thicker and bushier now, gets out his laptop, places it on the table, switches it on and raises his eyebrows slightly as he watches it fire up.

Tanya tries not to notice, but fails. He is still unbelievably gorgeous.

He starts typing, looking at the screen and not at Tanya.

Tanya's iPhone rings.

Kate: Are you busy, babes?

Tanya: *Babes!* You sound like you've been *crying!*

Kate: I have. Christina's turned out to be an absolute cunt. She's run off with some Italian bloke, can you fucking believe it?

Tanya: Noooo!

Kate: Yes!

Tanya: What a bitch!

Kate: I know.

Tanya: I thought she was meant to be super like metrosexually avant-garde or whatever.

Kate: She's a cunt.

Tanya: Well *that* is a real let down, Kate. Although I was suspicious when you showed me that photo of the henna tattoo on Christina's hand and I noticed the big chunky silver ring on her little finger, always a massive giveaway that a woman can't be trusted.

Kate: Where did you read that?

Tanya: I did a quiz on Buzzfeed. 'How trustworthy are you?' or something. Or maybe it was 'How trustworthy were you in a past life?'

Kate: Well she's turned out not to be trustworthy and I *hate* her. Look, I've got to go. Ring you back later OK?

Tanya: OK sweets. Miss you!

But Kate has gone.

As Tanya switches off her phone, she suddenly realises that the bloke with the beard has stopped typing and is now looking at her, studiously.

Bloke with the beard: Excuse me. I'm really sorry to interrupt you but I couldn't help overhearing you talking about *trustworthiness*.

Tanya: Yeeeees…

Bloke with the beard: Is it true? About chunky silver rings on little fingers?

Tanya: Well like I said, I don't know really, I just got it off a stupid Buzzfeed quiz…

Bloke with the beard: I saw one the other day called 'Which Ousted Arab Spring Leader Are You?'

Tanya: Did you do it?

Bloke with the beard: (laughing) I'm embarrassed to say, yes, I did.

Tanya: (laughing) And what did you get?

Bloke with the beard: Muammar Gaddafi.

Tanya: Well, he had a beard…

There's no doubt about it. He's hot and she still wants to fuck him. What would he think if he knew she'd already fantasised about him? Several times…

Tanya: So…what are you writing then, Gaddafi?

Bloke with the beard: A screenplay.

Tanya: I knew it! I saw you in here recently and thought 'He looks like a screenwriter.'

Bloke with the beard: I thought you looked familiar. I remember now. Didn't you drop your keys?

Tanya: Yes…so…what sort of screenplay is it?

Bloke with the beard: A rom-com. It's called 'How I Learnt to Understand Women.'

Tanya: Ah….

Bloke with the beard: Because of course, we can never understand you. You're all completely unfathomable…

As Tanya laughs in agreement, the bloke with the beard looks Tanya in the eyes and smiles. He's delicious. His eyes are actually melting a hole somewhere inside her.

Tanya: So what's your name?

Chris: Chris.

Tanya: Hi. I'm Tanya.

Chris: Hi Tanya.

Tanya: Funny, isn't it? What happens when you get talking to someone. When I saw you last time I was here, I thought you looked like you were a bit up yourself. But you're not…

Chris: And I thought your friend dropped her keys deliberately to see how I'd react. And such a presumptuous thought would make me a bit up myself. So maybe you were right…

Tanya: She did drop them deliberately. We'd been discussing you.

Chris: Really…

Tanya: Yeah. Well, Kate hadn't. I had…

Tanya looks Chris in the eyes with a long, even, look of desire which he returns. Neither of them look away. The look continues, second by second, as both realise that neither can look away. Time stands still, the rest of the world disappears and Tanya feels as though her heart is going to burst out of her chest.

After what must be more than a minute of looking intently at one another, Chris reaches over the table and gently grasps the tip of Tanya's little finger then slowly pulls her hand towards him, continuing to look her in the eye the whole time. He leans forward across the table and she in turn leans towards him. He gently takes her entire hand in his without squeezing it, and softly cups his other hand around the back of Tanya's neck, before leaning in and kissing her full on the lips…

A Passion for Classic Cars

28

ALEX AND SANDI AT WORK

amara, chignoned chestnut hair beautifully coiffured, nails manicured and make-up perfect, elegant in a smart navy linen trouser suit, puts her arms around Sandi as she stands outside the front entrance of Bates & Bartle in Soho Square on the verge of tears.

Tamara: Darling. Look. He's been a twat, really. Who does he think he is? Shagging you then completely ignoring you. And on top of living with his girlfriend. I don't want to hurt your feelings, but you deserve better. I've never really liked him to be honest. He seems so sure of himself. As though no-one else matters but him.

Sandi: Isn't that the default setting for every man in London?

Tamara: No. There are good ones out there. Believe me. Look at Tom. I know, I'm lucky...

Sandi: Tom is lovely, you're right.

Tamara holds her cigarette away from Sandi as she breaks away from the reassuring hug and exhales a plume of smoke with vigorous dissatisfaction. At Alex. At Sandi's stupidity. At the fact her fag break is being taken up with another Sandi counselling session.

Sandi: Give us a fag.

Tamara: You don't smoke! You told me you gave up years ago!
Sandi: I know. But I want one. Give me one, please.

Tamara reluctantly draws out a Marlboro light from her squishy soft pack and hands it to Sandi, passing her a lighter as well. Sandi lights the cigarette, inhales quickly then grimaces.

Sandi: God. I feel dizzy.
Tamara: Well you will, silly. You don't smoke!

Tamara throws the butt end of her cigarette onto the pavement and grinds it into the stone flag with her high, patent heel.

Tamara: Listen, I have to get back. I'll see you at lunch, OK?
Sandi: And thanks. Again.
Tamara: It's nothing. Love you, darling.
Sandi: You too.

As Tamara strides confidently back into the building, Sandi is left alone on the pavement, smoking and feeling awkward and totally alone. She can see a figure rounding the corner. It's Alex. He's late. Again. As he approaches her she notices that he looks as though he hasn't slept for a week. He stops when he reaches her, looking at her plaintively.

Sandi: You look terrible.
Alex: So do you. You're smoking. It doesn't suit you. Why are you smoking?
Sandi: Because I want to.
Alex: And you look like you've been crying.
Sandi: I have, Alex. Because you've been such a fucking shit. Alright?

Alex looks completely crestfallen, lowers his head and slumps down to sit, hunched, on the bottom step of the entrance way to B&B.

Alex: She's chucked me out. I mean, I've left her.

Sandi: What?

Alex: Well what did you expect after what you told her? You told her everything!

Sandi: For fuck's sake, Alex, she was about to find out anyway. Colin knew, Kate knew, it was only a matter of time before someone told Julia and I wanted it to come from me. I didn't want her hearing some distorted account from someone else who didn't know what the fuck they were talking about, OK? She needed to know that it was just a 'one-off' as you so charmingly described it.

Alex: Only it wasn't, Sandi. It wasn't a one-off. Well, I hope it wasn't...

Sandi: What do you mean?

Alex: I mean I hope it happens again.

Sandi: What, once again? So you can refuse to answer my texts and not turn up at work dos again because you're trying to avoid me?

Alex: No...that was just...circumstance. You've got to understand. Things have been very difficult for me. At home. Impossible, in fact. Living with my ex-wife's mother. Who's so interfering and boring. It's been a nightmare, actually.

Sandi: So you haven't actually been having sex regularly and you'd stopped actually fancying her. Is that it?

Alex: I haven't fancied her since I moved in.

Sandi: So you just enjoy the chase. Typical. At least now I know, Alex Harcourt.

Alex: It was her who chased me in the first place. I was vulnerable, at the end of a bad marriage to her spoilt brat of a daughter.

Sandi stubs out her cigarette on the floor. Alex stares at it.

Alex: I can't believe you're smoking. Couldn't you *vape*, or something?
Sandi: No, I couldn't '*vape or something*'. I cadged a fag because I fancied one. Because I can. And because I don't have anyone telling me what to do. And, Alex, I intend to continue that way. Independent. And single.

Sandi turns on her heels and marches into the building, seething with anger at what a complete dick Alex has been.
Once past reception, she looks out through the window and sees him sitting on the steps, looking fragile and forlorn, and her heart lurches. How can she not feel sympathy for him? His shoulders hunched, strands of curly brown hair flopping over his face, his lips slightly parted as though he's about to burst into tears at any moment.
She walks back outside into the warm sunshine and stands in front of Alex, who looks up at her, pitifully.

Sandi: I was going to go to lunch with Tamara. But I'll take you for lunch instead, OK? I think we have a lot of talking to do, don't you?
Alex: Thanks, yes, we do. That'd be nice. I just need to kind of find my bearings. I feel a bit lost at the moment.
Sandi: Well, you've found me now.

29

THE MILE HIGH CLUB

beria flight IB 3873 taxis on the runway and then takes off smoothly from the tarmac of Malaga airport. On the back row of the plane, Alessandro looks out of the window at the airport terminal building receding into the distance and the mountains beyond, and marvels at his luck. He went to Spain for adventure and he found it.

Christina adjusts the focus on the lens of her Nikon until Alessandro's head is perfectly sharp, a beatific smile on his face as he gazes out of the window. With his green, almond-shaped eyes, his dark brown hair softly curling over his neck and his olive skin, he is irresistible. Christina even finds his vanity and cocky arrogance amusing, she can sense that it's a thin shell covering a genuinely warm and gracious heart, one that she's prepared to follow back to his home city of Milan. She's always wanted to go to Milan, anyway, and there was no way she was going to stick around to stay with that spoilt, possessive brat, Kate. Alessandro encapsulates freedom, dreams and possibilities. His skin smells divine and she loves the way he fucks her. From where she's sitting in her airplane seat, he's got it all.

Alessandro feels the focus of Christina's lens on him, turns to look at her and smiles. She captures the shot.

'Let me see.'

Alessandro studies the shot of himself and nods sagely in appreciation.

'Put it down, now, Christina. I want to see you, not the camera.'

Christina puts the camera in her bag on the empty seat next to her then looks Alessandro in the eye. God, he's gorgeous.

The rows in front of them and on the other side of the aisle are both empty, the flight is only half full, and Christina is aware that now the air stewardesses have sat down at the front of the plane, they have privacy.

'Kiss me.' she demands, quietly.

Alessandro reaches out, holds Christina's shoulders, leans forward and half closes his eyes before kissing her deeply on the mouth, his tongue gently moving inside her mouth, immediately arousing her.

Christina slides her hand onto Alessandro's jeans, resting it on the top of his leg, near his crotch. She breaks off from the kiss and murmurs, her lips brushing against his,

'What are we going to do when we get back to Milan?'

'Fuck. We are going to fuck, Christina, every day and every night.'

Christina pulls back and looks into his eyes, slowly and evenly. She can feel herself hypnotised, drowning in their cat-like gaze and feels unbearably aroused. She shifts slightly in the upholstered aircraft seat.

Alessandro moves her hand onto the crotch of his jeans, which are raised by the bulge of his swollen erection beneath the fabric.

Christina massages the bulge with her hand and Alessandro moans, closing his eyes slightly

'I'm feeling unbelievably aroused, Alessandro.' she whispers.

Alessandro slides his hand along the bare skin of Christina's leg, starting just above her knee, moving his hand higher and higher up the silky skin of her thighs then slipping his fingers underneath her short skirt. He pushes his hand in between her legs and slides two fingers down over the silky fabric of her knickers, which are already soaking wet. Christina moans and he grins mischievously, rubbing his fingers back and forth over the fabric covering her pussy, first gently, then more firmly, building the strokes of his fingers into a regular rhythm.

Christina moves towards him again and kisses him deeply on the mouth, then breaks away, looks down at his crotch and unbuttons the flies of his jeans. She reaches inside. Alessandro is not wearing underpants, his cock is folded uncomfortably under the stiff fabric of his jeans. Christina grasps the shaft of his penis and springs it out from the sheaf of his trousers. His cock stands up stiffly and she glances up at him, smiling coquettishly as she holds it firmly in her hand, running her fingers lightly along its length, squeezing when she reaches the swollen head.

Alessandro leans over and kisses her again whilst maintaining a regular rhythm with his fingers, masturbating Christina's clitoris through the oily, sheer fabric.

Christina pulls down the foreskin of his penis to reveal the smooth, shiny, crimson head and then pushes the foreskin back up over the head. With deft strokes of her fingers, she grasps Alessandro's penis tightly and starts pumping it back and forth with regular strokes.

The aircraft no longer exists they are together in a world of their own. Alessandro gasps as he feels his orgasm rapidly approach, just the sense that he's about to come brings on Christina's own orgasm as her body spasms with waves of pleasure. She breaks off their deep, passionate kissing to watch Alessandro's penis spurt long streams of thick spunk, at first high above his head, the last few running over her hand.

Christina glances up and notices an stewardess approaching. Alessandro quickly puts his cock back into his jeans and buttons them up, struggling in the cramped seating. Christina slowly raises her eyes to the lighting above the seats - no sign of

Alessandro's spunk, she wonders where it ended up and can't help feeling incredibly naughty.

They both look at one another and burst out laughing. There is something about being with Alessandro that feels light and conspiratorial. Everything seems easy. Nothing is heavy, or complicated, or loaded. With him, she feels free.

Just as the sun is setting, the plane touches down in at Malpensa airport in Varese, just outside Milan. Five days here before Christina has to go back to Malaga to catch her return flight to London. She just hopes Kate's not on it. As soon as her mobile picks up the local network, her WhatsApp bleeps. Kate…

30

PARADISE IN HELL

rigiliana is now tainted with the stench of betrayal. Looking out from the terrace at the tiers of white houses nestled in the hillside, the beautiful brown and green terrain stretching out as far as the sea far below, Kate feels as if she's in a paradise in hell. Everyone she trusted has betrayed her. She was surrounded by utter twats back in England, she's flown here to escape them and still she's trapped by other people's foul deeds. Cunts, the lot of them!

Kate cancels her return ticket and buys another one so that she can fly back to the UK immediately.

She packs what little stuff she's brought and glances out at the terrace one more time before locking up. The sun mats lie there, bright and empty under the scorching sun. Kate's stomach churns at the thought of how she and Christina made love on them just the day before. Her eyes glance up to the window of the house opposite, overlooking the terrace, where, to rub salt into the wound of her desertion, those disgusting tourists were having sex near the open window in full public view yesterday as well. Who would even do that? Obscene. She wishes she'd been wearing her contact lenses so that she could have seen who it was and given them a filthy look the next time she was sitting in the cafe, in case they walked by. As it was, they were just a blur, but the noise was bad enough, the grunting and groaning. Sex is so base. Kate decides she might just become a nun and go and live in a monastery. If they'd have her.

In the long taxi ride on the way to Malaga airport, Kate suddenly becomes consumed with the anger she's been trying to run away from by coming out to Spain. As she thinks about all the people who have done her wrong, their selfishness makes her reel with self-justified loathing. She, Kate, has done nothing wrong. Ever. It's all their fault. Her mother. Alex. Matt. Christina. Even Colin has let her down. Which was unexpected.

She grabs her phone and starts messaging them all, one by one.

Mother. I know about you fucking my boyfriend. The second boyfriend you've stolen from me. You have deep psychological issues and need help. I don't want to see you until you start addressing them. Being a writer has obviously sent you over the edge and turned you into some kind of mad woman. Don't think I have any sympathy for you BECAUSE I DON'T. Matt is a selfish boring shit anyway just like Alex was so you're welcome to him. GOODBYE!!!

There. That feels *much* better.

Do you know what, Christina? When I first met you, I had respect for you. I thought you were sophisticated. But you're not. You're a tramp. And you're stupid, because you're a prostitute who doesn't get paid for it. Good riddance you can fuck right off, I hope I never see you again.

Better still, ha!

I know about you and my mother you utter cunt. Well she's old. And she's not getting any younger. You'll get bored. If you're wondering how I know, Colin told me. He's been fucking me since I met you so there you stupid wanker. Don't try and contact me EVER AGAIN!

Yeah. *Fuck off Matt!*

Already, Kate is starting to feel like a different person with these weights off her chest. Just Colin to go. He really could and should have come out to Frigiliana…

Look Colin, there's obviously been some sort of misunderstanding. I didn't mean to get angry with you the other day but you could have been a bit more helpful, yeah? I'm in a lot of pain out here you know, everyone's been shitting on me. I didn't expect you to be like them. Anyway look, I forgive you, let's put it behind us and I'll see you when I get back to London OK? xxx

As the plane taxis on the runway and takes off for England, Kate feels a huge sense of relief and quite proud of herself.

Finally, she's got rid of all the dead wood and is putting her life in order.

A Passion for Classic Cars

31

COLIN AND THE WOMAN AT GLOW

he terrace of Glow bar in Shoreditch is covered with dazzling yellow and white striped awnings, fluttering in the breeze. From his vantage point near the private forecourt in front of the bar, Colin can keep an eye on the motor, acquired just the week before, a black Bentley Continental GT V8, safely parked a few steps down from the terrace. Colin is now on his fifth margarita. It's 2pm.

A glacier white Bentley Continental GT3-R swings into view and parks up at the opposite side of the forecourt to Colin's.

A stunningly beautiful woman in her mid-thirties with long, wavy auburn hair, bright eyes and full lips leans forward, switches off the ignition and slinkily exits the car, long legs coated in sheer black tights and ending in perfect red high heels with red soles. Laboutins. She's wearing a tight red skirt suit comprising of box jacket and a pencil skirt. She's Joan Holloway out of *Mad Men*. She's a perfect, shimmering vision of loveliness and she knows it, but also carries with her an air of modesty which makes her doubly entrancing.

Rather than immediately sashaying up the entrance steps to the terrace, she stands still momentarily, casting her eyes up at all the people sitting at tables deliberately feigning indifference to her. Only a toddler in his buggy stares in her direction, intrigued.

She smiles to herself on seeing the familiar face for which she was looking, the waiter, Julius, and begins her walk up the steps of judgement. No-one turns their head, but plenty of eyes furtively glance momentarily at her before looking quickly away, not wanting to be seen to notice her. This is London, where you go out to be seen, not to be seen to look...

Shelley walks over to the nearest vacant table, a stripped pine affair decorated with a small jam jar of wild flowers next to a yellow glass ash tray, in which has been stubbed a white cigarette end stamped with pink lipstick.

Before she has a chance to sit down, Julius sees her and rushes over, throwing his arms around her. Five foot five, with short sandy blonde hair, a closely cropped beard and smiling blue eyes, he has the air of a kindly ferret about him.

'Shelley! Darling! It's been weeks!'

Shelley returns his embrace, warmly.

'I've been on tour, I told you, remember?'

'On *tour!* Oh yes, you *did!* You know I've got a brain like a sieve. It was Europe, right?'

'Correct. Germany, Luxembourg and Denmark...'

'Denmark, oh Denmark! Darling! I'd so *love* to go to Copenhaaaaagen.' says Julius, dragging out the 'a'. 'How was it?'

'Divine. Wonderful place, wonderful people.'

'Fabulous! I need to find a lovely little *Dane* who'll keep me warm at nights and take me over to his place in Copenhaaaaagen! What can I get you? The usual?'

'I'm driving. A chilled bottle of Evian would be lovely. Ice and lime.'

Julius sweeps up the used ashtray with a swift gesture of his hand and blows Shelley a kiss.

'Right away, sweets.'

Colin and the Woman at Glow

Colin, sitting at the next table and feigning disinterest by punching text into his Samsung Galaxy with both hands, feels like puking into his margarita. What a fucking *tosser!*

His phone bleeps the bird whistle tone with an incoming message. Kate. Yeah, blah blah blah blah blah *'I'll see you when I get back to London OK?'* Whatever.

Shelley winces slightly at the ubiquitous bird whistle tone from the next table as she scrolls through her iPhone 6 Plus, picking up on the book she's reading, Dr. Nafeez Ahmed's *A User's Guide to the Crisis of Civilization: And How to Save It.* She glances up to see where the irritating tone is coming from. Colin catches her eye and grins.

'Couldn't help noticing the motor.'

Shelley says nothing, but looks at him, evenly. The bank clerk hair. The smarmy smirk. Creep.

'Same as mine. Mine's the black one, over there.' Colin gestures with a flick of his wrist. 'Bentley Continental, yeah?'

'Correct.' says Shelley, flatly.

'Bought mine last week. Mine's higher spec than yours, though. 528 horsepower at 6000 reveroonies..'

Shelley glances over at Colin's car.

'That's a GT V8 S.'

'Correct, babes.'

'Don't call me 'babes'.'

'*Chillax.* You're gorgeous. And so is your motor. Like mine.'

'As I said, yours is a GT V8 S...' snaps Shelley, coldly.

'And yours is a...'

'GT3-R. Limited edition of 300. Mine's number 36.'

'It doesn't make 528 horsepower though...'

'Mine actually does *580* horsepower flat out at 6000 revs per minute and *516* pounds of torque just when it's ticking over at 1700 revs.'

'Oh, I see. You're one of those *feminist petrolheads*.' sneers Colin, acidly.

'It's not only more powerful than the GT V8 S but it's got torque vectoring for each of the rear wheels, shorter gearing, recalibrated control software, all-new titanium exhaust with a 7 kg weight saving and retuned acoustics. Plus it's 100kg lighter than yours. Shall I go on?'

'Well memorised. You've done your homework. So who bought it for you?'

'I bought it myself.'

'Ooooh…clever as well as beautiful.'

'You know, I came here alone. I didn't ask for you or any other man to talk to me or pass judgement on my looks, my car or my brains. For the first one minute after I arrived, I was quite happy reading my book and waiting for my drink.'

'Yeah I saw. iPhone 6 Plus. They bend in your trouser pocket when you sit down.'

'I don't use a *trouser pocket*.'

Julius sails into view bearing aloft a silver tray with a bottle of Evian and a glass full of ice with a couple of slices of lime. He swoops the bottle and glass in front of Shelley and grins.

'I finish at 4. Fancy going to Paolo's for one? Oh no, you're driving!'

'I can ring George to pick the car up for me. Yes, actually, I do fancy going to Paolo's.'

Shelley glares at Colin, raising her eyebrows slightly. 'You're not going to follow us, I hope…'

'Not my kind of place, babes. Full of hipsters sitting around posing…I'm a bit above that…'

Julius completely ignores Colin, winks at Shelley and sails off again.

Shelley looks around her, at the happy couples talking, silent couples each on their phones, the single men, single women, the mother wiping ice cream from the toddler's face over there, the groups of business acquaintances talking animatedly, and marvels that she's ended up sitting next to this utter bell-end. He's tried to belittle her several times. Talked down to her and patronised her in a manner to which she's become accustomed, day in, day out by various men just by dint of her being a woman. Dick.

Colin swigs the last of his margarita and sulkily gets up from his seat, stumbling slightly. He leaves enough money on the table to pay the bill and takes one last look at this bird who would be gorgeous if she weren't so completely up herself.

Shelley smiles broadly at him.

'Look, please don't think I was being rude, you took me by surprise, that was all. I love your car. And I love talking about cars, as you've seen. Maybe we could meet up somewhere for a drink at the weekend, you know, in our respective cars? I'd love that.'

Colin's face lights up. She's not up her own arse after all!

'Alright. Yeah, why not?'

Shelley takes a blank business card from her purse, on which is scrawled a mobile phone number in pencil. She leans forward exposing the slightest bit of cleavage from her tight, white blouse, and hands the card to Colin.

'My personal number. That's the one I always answer. Give me a ring soon.'

'Cool.'

Colin trots down the steps to the forecourt and strides cockily over to his car, managing to walk in a straight line, unlocks the car from a distance with his remote key, then climbs in and drives off, tyres screeching.

⁂⁂⁂

Colin doesn't ring Shelley for a week. When he dials the number on his phone, +44 20 3095 4193, he gets this recorded message:

'Sometimes people try to destroy you, precisely because they recognise your power, not because they don't see it, but because they do see it and they don't want it to exist.'

He should have known it. What a cunt.

The End

Engraving by Borel and Elluin for John Cleland's
A Woman of Pleasure ~ 1776

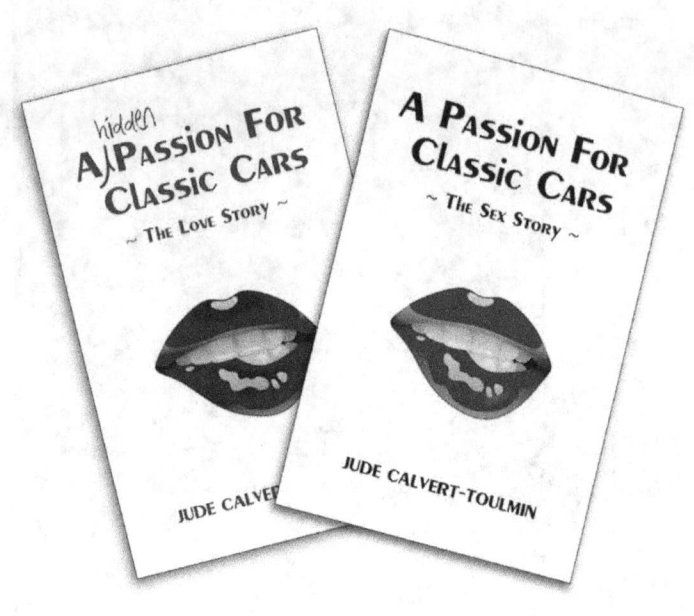

Also available without the sex scenes as
A Hidden Passion for Classic Cars

Credits

Author – Jude Calvert-Toulmin
Editor – Brian Trevelyan
Typesetting – Fleur de Lys
Cover design - Jude Calvert-Toulmin
Vintage Erotique Font - Darrian Lynx
Computer consultant - Andy Milne

Jude Calvert-Toulmin Novels

Labrats

The Willow Tree Trilogy:
My Adventures in Cyberspace
Drowning
The Moonbeam (forthcoming)

The Julia Books:
Mother-in-Law, Son-in-Law
A Passion for Classic Cars
A Hidden Passion for Classic Cars

www.judecalverttoulmin.com
www.fleurdelyspublishing.com